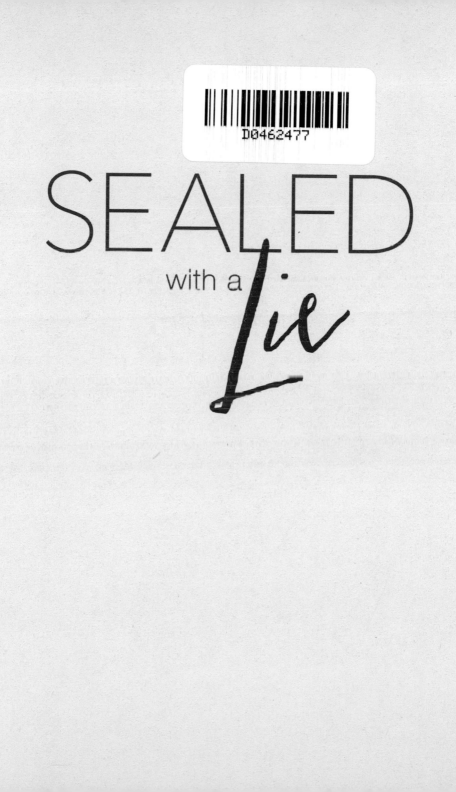

SEALED
with a *Lie*

ALSO BY KAT CARLTON

Two Lies and a Spy

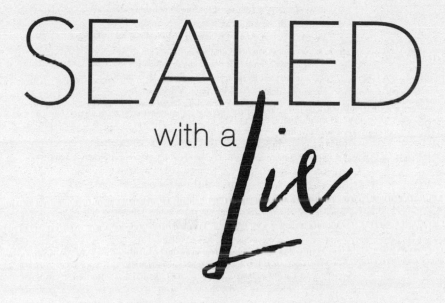

SEALED
with a *Lie*

KAT CARLTON

SIMON & SCHUSTER BFYR

New York   London   Toronto   Sydney   New Delhi

An imprint of Simon & Schuster Children's Publishing Division
1230 Avenue of the Americas, New York, New York 10020

For information about special discounts for bulk purchases, please contact Simon & Schuster
Special Sales at 1-866-506-1949 or business@simonandschuster.com.
The Simon & Schuster Speakers Bureau can bring authors to your live event.
For more information or to book an event, contact the Simon & Schuster Speakers Bureau
at 1-866-248-3049 or visit our website at www.simonspeakers.com.
Also available in a SIMON & SCHUSTER BFYR hardcover edition
Book design by Krista Vossen
The text for this book is set in Berling LT Std.
Manufactured in the United States of America
First SIMON & SCHUSTER BFYR paperback edition September 2015
2 4 6 8 10 9 7 5 3 1
The Library of Congress has cataloged the hardcover edition as follows:
Carlton, Kat.
Sealed with a lie / Kat Carlton.
pages cm
Sequel to: Two lies and a spy.
Summary: At the bidding of a voice on a phone, sixteen-year-old Kari
and her friends from Generation Interpol, a spy training facility, race around Europe
to fulfill a list of demands, as Kari's brother's life hangs in the balance.
ISBN 978-1-4814-0052-7 (hc)
[1. Spies—Fiction. 2. Europe—Fiction.] I. Title.
PZ7.C216852Se 2014
[Fic]—dc23
2013041857
ISBN 978-1-4814-0053-4 (pbk)
ISBN 978-1-4814-0054-1 (eBook)

To the Muse. I figure if I thank you
publicly, maybe you'll return to visit!

Acknowledgments

A huge thank-you to David Valys, triple black belt in three martial arts that I cannot begin to pronounce, who helped me choreograph the opening scene of this book. And to Dr. Art Rich, PhD, who generously shared his knowledge of cosmetic chemistry and corporate laboratory security, without once laughing at my ridiculous questions! Thanks as well to my friends Sarah Strock and Kathryn de Palo, who came up with an ingenious solution to a plot issue, and to Claudio Cambon for his help with French. Thanks to readers in advance for allowing me to invent a juvenile detention center in Murnau, toss a fictitious parking garage onto a street in Munich where none exists, make free with train stops, create a Schiff boathouse on the Salzach River—and a few other little details like that! Finally, I owe a big debt of gratitude to Dani Young and the whole team at Simon & Schuster, without whom this book would not exist.

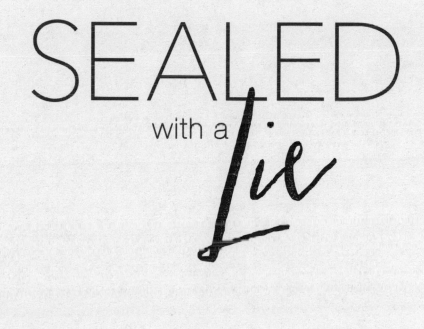

Chapter One

There's a six-foot man in front of me whom I need to put six feet under.

I may not be able to go through him physically, but I *will* disable him and get around him—even if he blocks my opening moves.

"Not bad, little girl," he says with a smirk playing on his insufferable, arrogant British mouth.

Little girl? I can almost feel sparks shooting down my spine. My blood boils, and adrenaline tingles in my legs. I almost levitate with sheer aggression.

This little girl's gonna take you down.

Despite his condescending, obnoxious words, the normally calm, cool Evan Kincaid is perspiring, and I can smell the damp, musky heat of his body instead of his designer deodorant. His mocking gray-blue eyes have darkened with focus, and his alert, carefully loose stance tells me that he's taking me seriously.

It's about time. My job is to take him out, and fast.

I crouch lower, weight on the balls of my feet, and he warily adjusts his own stance. As I size him up, though, I note that his arms are too low . . . a sign of cockiness. He's confident that he's going to beat me—why? I know karate as well as he does. Better, in fact.

Evan is tall, but not beefy. He's tough and cut and moves with a sinewy grace. Because of his superior height, he's got about seven inches more arm reach than I do, and twelve inches of additional leg reach. This means that his "ma" distance, or effective sphere of control, is much larger than mine. He'll want to take advantage of that, using kicks.

Since he outweighs me by seventy pounds, I can't go to the ground with him unless it's a finishing move. I'll need to close that "ma" gap, or I'll be in trouble.

Evan sizes me up the same way that I evaluate him, gauging my strengths and weaknesses. Will he wait for me to move first this time?

No. He launches a series of spinning kicks: a front kick, followed by a spinning heel, then a roundhouse.

I step out of range of the first, then barely out of range of the second. But I can't avoid him forever. Eventually, Evan will connect.

I move in on number three, blocking his right knee with my left palm to stop the kick. I punch the instep of his extended foot hard with my right hand, a move called "oi-tsuki."

Yes!

Evan winces and gives an audible gasp. Two white dents appear on either side of his nostrils. His eyes narrow on me.

A smirk crosses my face. Evan deserves it, just as he deserves the nasty bruise he'll develop at his instep. Evan is the reason I'm stuck in Paris.

I focus for a fleeting moment on his mouth and how it felt pressed against mine when he backed me against a wall and stole my first kiss.

Jerk.

Slimeball.

Egomaniac.

I press my advantage, launching myself at Evan just as he is forced to put weight on his injured foot.

I dive-roll past his kicking range and come up to deliver a flurry of punches centerline.

If there's any justice in this world, I'll connect.

But he blocks each blow in turn—I'm not even sure how. His hands are a blur. Worse, he catches my last punch, knocks me off-balance, and pulls me forward into a throw.

Unexpectedly, I'm flying.

But I've trained long and hard.

I roll out of the throw and come swiftly to my feet, turning to face him in a stance.

Except he's not where I expect him to be.

What the—?

Oh, no.

What was that I mentioned about him being cocky? I've made the same mistake.

Evan's left arm snakes out and circles my neck. His right arm locks behind my head, squeezing my carotid artery. I struggle to free myself using every tactic I can think of—feet, elbows, hands, hips. I stomp, claw, shove, and even try to bite him as I get ever more desperate.

But he's relentless.

He uses his bicep and forearm to shut off my blood flow. . . .

And I can't breathe. As I strain to free myself, every bad word I know flashes neon in my head. None of them can quite express the depth of my feelings.

Evan chuckles softly.

This little girl's not taking him down, not by a long shot. If he wanted to, he could jerk me higher and wring my neck like a chicken's. How could I have let him get the advantage like this?

"Relax, darling," he murmurs. "Make your peace with sudden death."

I make one last, futile attempt to drive an elbow backward into his six-pack abs. It takes every iota of energy I have left, and it accomplishes absolutely nothing.

Evan's chest rumbles against my spine. Is he *purring*?

My vision blurs, then fades—though I can still see the *F* word emblazoned in flaming letters behind my eyelids. Maybe they'll engrave it on my tombstone after they bury me.

Hate. Evan. Kincaid.

And he *so* doesn't merit being the focus of my last conscious thoughts.

In the end, I'm not sure who I'm madder at—myself,

for being so careless, or him, for choking the life out of me.

Before I can decide, everything goes black.

I regain consciousness within seconds and realize that Evan has let me down gently onto the thick blue mat of GI's studio. All around us are walls of mirrors that have reflected and refracted my total humiliation a hundredfold. My palms lie sweaty against the scuffed vinyl, and the air in my nostrils is thick with the dirty, plasticky scent of it.

I open my eyes and expect to see Evan towering over me, a six-foot, *gi*-clad exclamation point at the tail end of my mortification. I'm half-relieved but somehow half-disappointed that he's not. Then I'm mad at myself for the half-disappointed part. *What* is my problem?

"Kari? You okay?" asks Sensei Joe. He extends a hand to help me up.

"I'm fine," I mumble, and struggle upright, ignoring the hand. Evan is across the room, standing near the door and surrounded by an adoring gaggle of girls. He shoots a sympathetic glance in my direction, and his mouth twists in something like an apology.

Oooooh. Seriously? After just decimating me, he doesn't get to play Mr. Nice Guy now! He can stuff his sympathy where the sun don't shine.

There are whispers and low laughter and sidelong glances from the other students in the class as they filter out of the room. I wish Evan could choke off my embarrassment just like he did my oxygen. Why did I have to regain consciousness? I feel a flush spreading over my face and neck.

Sour grapes have yielded sweet wine for the others. I've beaten them all, every student in Generation Interpol, including Evan—until today. That's why they're thrilled that he's outmaneuvered me. He is their hero.

Hoo-rah.

I can't believe I've lost this fight. Out of arrogance. Thinking that I was invincible. I cringe.

Though I try telling myself that I'm just off my game, the unpleasant truth bites me in the butt and won't let go. Evan is better than I am. Not just bigger and stronger, but better. Clearly he's been holding something back until today, which enrages me. He's been letting me win—setting me up to take a fall.

I stomp into the girls' locker room, aware of snickers behind my back. Cecily Alarie, the girl they call "Roux," curls her lip and laughs openly as she bends over and twists a towel into a turban around her wet copper-red hair.

GI may be in Paris, the City of Light, but this is the darkest time of my life. It may be full of geniuses and agents-in-training; it may be the ticket to an exciting life of fighting global crime, but it sucks.

It's tough to have a sunny outlook on life when the parents I idolized have turned traitors and shamed not only me, but the Agency and their country. They took some getaway jet to Russia and left me and my brother behind . . . to the tender mercy of the US foster-care system. We were able to avoid it only because of my unusual skill set—and my brother's.

Seven-year-old Charlie is a budding genius who speaks several languages and will probably win the Nobel Prize one day. I have some talent for karate and a broad base of knowledge that includes an ability to pick locks, "borrow" cars, and rock disguises.

We are stuck in France with Evan Kincaid and his group of international wankers at the Paris Institute during regular school hours. Once the bell rings, we attend GI, which kids who are not in the know refer to as "Get In." They think it's a fast track to admission at top colleges all over the world.

It really stands for Generation Interpol, a daily after-school training program for kids who've been hand-selected to become spies. The cherry on top? I never wanted to be a spy, and I don't speak French. Judging by my recent test scores (despite studying for hours), I never will. The only French word I know is *douche*. I call Evan that a lot. But who turned out to be the douche today? Me.

Cecily (I privately call her Madame de Pompadour, who was Top Ho to one of the ugly French king Louises) smirks at me as I peel off my damp, dirty *gi*, then shove it into my locker and slam the door. I quickly wrap a towel around my angular, boyish naked body and head for the showers.

As if she knows my insecurities, Cecily drops the towel from her own body, and I am treated to the sight of her curves as she steps into a pair of lacy silk electric-blue tap pants. I'm sorry to say that she is a natural redhead and has large, perfect breasts. She will stuff those into a matching electric-blue boob holster that's slung casually over her gym bag. No wonder Evan had a special friendship with her . . . one with benefits. Ugh.

I avert my eyes, but not quickly enough. She says something to her two sidekicks in French that I don't understand, and they all laugh. I feel their eyes burning my backside as I scurry off, holding the towel tightly around myself.

Why is there a girl like Cecily in every school? I have escaped Lacey Carson, my old nemesis from Kennedy Prep, only to face an even worse version of her. At least Lacey didn't prance around naked in front of me—she had the courtesy to wear a plaid miniskirt, part of our school uniform. And she was reassuringly American and therefore not all that mysterious.

Madame de Pompadour and her ladies-in-waiting are so Parisian that it's painful. They're not just garden-variety obnoxious. They're chic and sophisticated about it. They ooze French from their pores.

I feel bland and uninteresting in comparison, like a human bowl of grits.

With a sudden pang, I miss my best friend Rita, with her fabulous wardrobe and full array of coordinating designer eyeglasses. I wonder what she's up to, back in Washington, DC. I miss my other best friend Kale, too. I wonder if they've been allowed to see each other since we all got into so much trouble at the Agency?

I *really* miss my boyfriend, Luke. It's been hard dating long-distance.

I almost hack up a hair ball thinking about it, but I even miss Lacey, his sister. At least she could give me makeup tips, so that I could camouflage myself around Cecily.

I drape my towel on a hook near the shower, turn on the faucet, and step under the spray of hot water. Before I realize it, tears are running down my face, and I'm in full-on self-pity mode. This disgusts me, so paradoxically, I cry harder. My only comfort is that nobody can tell, since water is water, whether it comes out of an eye or a nozzle.

For the first time in my life, I feel like a total loser.

I've felt dumb before. I've felt awkward and occasionally unattractive. Who hasn't? But I've never felt this dull ache, this hopelessness, this loneliness that rolls over me on the flip side of my anger at my parents, at Evan, at *everything*.

Distracted by my dark thoughts, I slip on the slick communal shower floor and almost wipe out. I look down and see that somebody's squirted a good six-inch lake of conditioner or lotion right at my feet. It's been done deliberately to make me fall. Cecily?

I hose it down the drain and kick the tiled wall, which hurts but makes me feel better.

I am *not* a loser.

Nobody here is going to make me feel this way. And I will learn French if it kills me . . . if only so that I can effectively insult all these Generation Interpol snots. They may never like me, but they *will* respect me.

Chapter Two

Oh, joy. The only GI class I hate more than French is Tech 101. I can barely manage to xerox my own butt on a copy machine.

Why do I need to know how to dismantle and reassemble a cell phone? Much less create a scrambler for one? You tell me. But here I sit, surrounded by the parts of a cheap iPhone knockoff. It's no mystery how to take out the SIM card—even I can do that—but now we have to become electrical engineers? Jeez!

Jean-Paul Olivier, the instructor, has a mop of graying dark hair and small, very pale blue eyes. He wears pants that are too big for him, a shirt with a slightly frayed collar, and a shabby blazer that reeks of BO. He carries a battered leather man-purse. At the moment, he's jabbering away in incomprehensible French.

Ignoring the scattered plastic and metal parts in front

of me, I sneak my hand into my backpack and fish out my own cell phone. I text my karate buddy Kale. *Paris blows . . . everyone here sucks. How r u?*

I wish I could text Rita, but after hacking into the Agency director's laptop, she's been banned from all technical devices for six months. It's got to be killing her.

Kale himself can't be too happy, since he's been barred for an equal amount of time from any martial arts classes—punishment for helping me incapacitate several Agency employees.

I surreptitiously slide the phone back into its pocket and pretend to listen to the lecture.

Nobody seems to care that I don't speak Frog. The attitude is that they will "immerse" me and I will eventually learn the language out of desperation. Would these people toss a toddler into the Seine without arm floaties? Tell the kid to sink or swim?

I can't follow what the professor is saying, and unconsciously I zone out, following the movement of his Adam's apple as it bobs up and down. He has missed a tiny patch of bristle under his chin while shaving. It looks goofy. Olivier's teeth look like dejected prisoners jumbled together in a very small jail cell, straining to get out. I wonder if he's ever seen a dentist.

My attention wanders from Olivier's physical appearance to the parameters of the room we're in. Generation Interpol is housed in an old, gray stone beaux arts building with soaring arches everywhere. It's chilly, cluttered with neoclassical sculpture, and reminds me a lot of the Library of Congress in Washington, DC.

Frankly, it's weird to be studying cutting-edge tech-nology while surrounded by goddesses and scantily clad nymphs and half-naked warriors with spears. I'm check-ing out the winged sandals on a figure of Hermes and wishing I had a pair that would fly me away from here when Olivier notices me daydreaming.

"*Kahrri? 'Allo? Kah-rrhhii!*" He barks my name, mak-ing the *r* sound like bile clawing its way up his throat.

I blink. "Uh, oui, Monsieur Olivier?"

"*Blah blah blah blah le telephone!*"

"Uh . . ." I have no idea what the man just said. It's heavily accented gibberish.

"*Vite, Kahrri, vite!*" That means "quickly."

I open and close my mouth like a fish. I look down at the scattered phone parts on my desk. "Huh?"

Two desks ahead of mine, Cecily turns her head, mur-murs something, and gives a delicate snort. Her cohorts sneer through their pale, understated lip gloss.

Olivier repeats whatever it is that he jabbered at me.

I stare helplessly at him.

"*Mon Dieu,*" he exclaims, and rolls his eyes, the whites showing. He shakes his head and makes another mysteri-ous Gallic pronouncement.

Why does it have to be Evan who comes to my rescue? "Kari, he wants you to slip the listening device into the phone and then reassemble it. *Comprends-tu?*"

I'm torn between gratitude, embarrassment, and irrita-tion. I nod my thanks at him before muttering, "You know this is dumb, right? There's easily downloadable spyware on the Internet that can monitor any cell phone." I know this from Rita, the hacker and gadget expert. What I don't know is how it works, exactly.

So Olivier, who evidently has ears like a bat, invites me to explain it to the entire class, of course. In French.

I glare at him, doubly handicapped.

He waves his hand magnanimously and gives me a charming smile. *"Karrhi? S'il vous plait."*

"It's keystroke-monitoring software," Evan announces. "Absolutely undetectable. Allows you to view your target's contact list, outgoing and incoming calls, listen to what's being said, and view texts, even deleted ones."

"Vraiment?" Olivier asks, feigning utter fascination. *"Formidable!"*

A tight ball of dread has formed in my gut. I have a bad feeling I know what's coming next.

"One can view texts?" Olivier marvels. "Ah . . . perhaps like zis?" He saunters over to the laptop on his podium, minimizes his PowerPoint presentation, and taps a few keys.

"'Paris blows . . . ,'" he announces, bringing my text to Kale up onto the screen in front of the class. *"'Everyone here sucks.'"*

Oh, dear God. As if this day hasn't already been bad enough? I slide down in my seat.

"'How r u?'" Olivier inquires sardonically.

My pulse is thundering in my ears. I can feel a hot red flush burning the skin of my face and neck. *Somebody just kill me now . . . please?*

"Karrhhi?"

"I'm sorry," I mutter.

"*Pardon?*"

I stare down at my desk. "I'm sorry."

"*En Francais, Karrhhi. En Francais!*"

At this point, I'm wishing that Evan had choked me out for good this morning. To my horror, more tears are trying to fight their way into my eyes. I would sooner die than lose it in front of this shabby sadist, in front of the whole class. I bite down, hard, on my tongue and relish the pain.

"*Karrhhi?*"

"That's enough," Evan says. "Leave her alone." He says it in French, but I put two and two together from the tone of his voice, the outraged response from Olivier at being given orders by a student, and the gestures both of them make at each other. Evan gets up from his chair, advances on the smaller man, and stares him down while the interchange escalates into a shouting match.

I want to crawl under my desk and dig a hole to China, but Tech 101 doesn't provide the tools to do that. So I'm forced to watch as Evan is ordered from the room and sent to Generation Interpol's version of the principal's office . . . for my sake.

Check in the dictionary next to the word "misery," and you will find my picture. Evan, who destroyed my pride and deprived me of oxygen just this morning, has now become my hero. But I don't know what to do with that . . . and I'm envious that he's escaped class while I'm still stuck here.

I inhale the stink of everyone's hatred. My text hasn't

helped things, and somehow they think it's my fault that Evan's in trouble—even though I didn't ask him to stand up for me.

I wrestle with another truth. I don't really despise Evan Kincaid.

I just wish I did.

It would be so much easier if I loathed him. Then I wouldn't be confused, and I wouldn't remember exactly how his body felt against mine when he had me in that choke hold. I wouldn't have felt the vibrations of his voice so deeply in my own chest. I wouldn't still remember the scent of him—laundry soap, a woodsy aftershave, and a hint of musk.

What is wrong with me? I am *totally* in love with my boyfriend. It's just the long-distance thing that's getting to me. I know that.

I fight the urge to pull out my cell phone again and stare at a picture of Luke. If I do that, Olivier will (no doubt) flash it up on the screen in front of the class and mock me until I spontaneously combust.

Oddly enough, Olivier seems to have taken Evan's shouted orders under advisement, since he ignores my existence for the rest of the class. I do my best to understand what he's saying, and I play monkey-see, monkey-do: watching and mimicking the kids around me as they reassemble the cell phone with the bug in it.

We then disassemble the phone once again and remove the bug. Then Olivier demonstrates the downloadable keystroke software that Evan explained. He also, thank God, shows us how to set the phones back to factory settings and get rid of his horrible spyware. I've learned a painful lesson.

I guess Evan knew more about all of this because he's been in the field longer than the rest of us. Evan's been in Generation Interpol since he was thirteen. His parents are dead, not just disgraced like mine. I wonder what that's like . . . the awful finality of it. The realization that he's completely alone in the world.

I shiver. I'm so lucky that I have my brother, Charlie. And when this awful tech class ends, I'll go pick him up and hug him tight. He's the only good thing in my life, in Paris, and in Generation Interpol.

Charlie is a small miracle. I couldn't survive without him.

Charlie sits with his tutor Clearance Matthis in a computer lab, two geeks on cloud nine.

Charlie looks like a miniature banker in his khakis, blue oxford-cloth button-down shirt, loafers, and horn-rims. Matthis, who's my age, wears cobalt-blue metallic-framed glasses, a moth-eaten gray sweater, faded jeans, and neon-green track shoes. He's super skinny, but he must have a tapeworm, because the boy eats like an ox—I have seen him inhale two lunches and a massive slab of cake within about eighty-five seconds.

At the moment, his chocolate-brown face glows eerily in the green light of twin computer screens. Charlie's pale face, only inches away, looks ghostly. The two have the lights turned low in the lab so that they can see better. And oddly enough, they both have identical pairs of sunglasses next to their keyboards.

Sunglasses? It's a cloudy, rainy day in Paris. Why would they need shades? And especially inside?

They're so intent on the computers that they don't even notice my arrival, and their expressions are rapt. Almost worshipful. I have a fleeting moment of terror that perhaps Matthis has introduced my little brother to porn.

I sneak up behind the boys just to make sure and yell, "Boo!"

Matthis jumps three feet out of his chair and comes down in a tangle of flying limbs, hyperventilating.

Charlie only lifts a pale blond eyebrow. "You're so immature."

"I know." At sixteen, I love being told that by a seven-year-old. "Can't help myself. What are you guys up to?"

"This is so cool. Matthis saw these sunglasses on the Internet and developed his own prototype!" Charlie waves his pair. "And guess what they do?"

I open my mouth to say something irreverent, but he doesn't wait for an answer.

"They take pictures! And video!"

"Really?" I'm intrigued. "How?"

"You just touch the logo on the left—it's a button—and it takes still photos. Press the one on the right for video. Then you turn your head and look at whatever you want to record. The images get stored here"—he points to the stems of the glasses—"in tiny hidden flash drives. And then you can download them to your computer."

"Wow," I say. "That's very cool." I turn to Matthis. "And you built these? Yourself?"

He's recovered from his fright. He bobs his head shyly. "You rock, Matthis!"

He blushes, stares at the floor, then folds his long legs up in a Buddha position, rolling office chair and all. That takes a certain amount of talent and balance all by itself, and I tell him so. He blushes again—it's hard to see because his skin is so dark, but I can tell, even in the low lighting. He casts about for something to do so that he won't have to meet my eyes and settles for snatching off his glasses and cleaning them on his sweater.

Matthis is one of the shyest people I've ever met. It's sort of endearing, though. I don't know him that well, partly because Charlie and I have been here only a couple of months and partly because the dude doesn't speak. But his dad is the janitor at the GI building, and I suspect he has a complex about that—even though his mom is the top analyst at GI and that alone should make him proud.

Anyway. I try to draw Matthis out of his shell whenever I can. Not that it's so easy.

"So, Matthis. Show me a video that you've made with these wild sunglasses."

He jams his glasses back onto his nose, then exchanges a glance with Charlie, who nods. Why am I suddenly uneasy?

With a few strokes on his keyboard, Matthis brings up an image of my face on his screen. My face and the back of Evan's head. As the camera pans out, it reveals that we're in our *gis*. Matthis pushes the play button.

"Seriously?" I query.

The two boys giggle, and I am forced to relive my humiliating defeat at Evan's hands. It's very weird to see the combination of aggression and arrogance on my own mug, and excruciating to witness the moment when it changes to shock and then mortification. Worse, I realize that I look like a rag doll that the Invincible Evan is toying with.

I cringe; now it's my turn to blush. But the two boys don't notice—they're too pleased with their coup at my expense. Nice.

"Thanks for that," I say breezily. "And I'm *fine* by the way—thanks for asking."

"Oh, we knew that," Charlie announces. "Evan would never hurt you. I mean, not really."

Now I'm offended. "He made me pass out! You don't think that's hurting me?"

"Nah."

"Wow, Charlie. You're pretty callous, don't you think?"

"Nope," my little brother says. "Evan let go right away, and he looked like he'd do CPR on you in a heartbeat if necessary."

"Totally," Matthis agrees.

"Huh." I swallow and try very hard not to think about that. *Luke, Luke, why won't you come visit?* I know all I need is to see him in person, and this strange thing with Evan will go away.

I'm starting to wonder if I'm becoming a bad person . . . OMG, what if I turn out like my parents? The whole "blood will tell" thing? That doesn't bear thinking about.

Even though I know stuff like this is not preordained—I

have control over the kind of person I become—anxiety floods my system. I feel as if ants are crawling over my body, doing little jigs on my skin. I need to get out of this building and away from anyone and anything in GI. The very last place I want to be right now is in spy school! Learning to be just like Mom and Dad. *Ugh.*

"C'mon, Charlie," I say, as casually as I can manage. "I hate to cut this short, but we need to be going."

His face falls, and so does Matthis's. "You guys can't hang out for a while?"

I open my mouth to refuse, but they make big, sad puppy eyes at me. *Aaargggh.* I am desperate for air and just want to be outside on the street. "We really do have to be going . . . but how about if we stop on the way home for hot chocolate? With extra whipped cream?"

There's an amazing little chocolate café a couple of blocks away. It looks like an old-fashioned tearoom, but they specialize in hot cocoa and pastries. It's a little bit girlie, but Charlie loves anything on the menu and so chooses to ignore the feminine surroundings.

"Yeah!" he says with glee.

I turn to Matthis, who looks hangdog. "Hey, you want to join us?"

He nods, his expression breaking my heart. It's as if he's fearful that I'm going to take back the invitation, that it's too good to be true. Poor Matthis. I don't think anyone ever really asks him to do anything fun.

"Well, c'mon already," I nudge him.

He almost trips over his own feet as he jumps up, wraps the prototypes of the sunglasses in soft chamois cloth, then starts to stuff them into his backpack.

"Hey," Charlie says. "Why don't we wear them and video stuff?"

So they do. As we hit the streets of Paris, I'm unwillingly drawn to the beauty, architecture, and history of the city, while they video passersby, dogs in cafés, pigeons, and even a newspaper page that's being blown along the sidewalk.

I wrestle—not too hard—with my moodiness while acknowledging a cool thing about Paris: It's willing, especially on a gray December day like this one, to be moody right along with me.

The boys video the chocolate shop's display window, the stairs, the menu, and the waitress. And after we've gorged ourselves on *pain au chocolat* and *chocolat chaud* (hot chocolate), Charlie begs to borrow the pair of sunglasses he's wearing, just for the night. He swears to return them the next day. Matthis is clearly tickled that Charlie loves them so much, so he agrees.

Oh, boy. I guess Charlie will be taking video of the Metro station, the tracks, and the train, too . . . somehow, I manage to contain my excitement.

Chapter Three

The Paris Metro is not nearly as clean as the Metro in DC. I make Charlie hold my hand, even though he's offended that I still treat him like a baby and he feels that it's "entirely unnecessary." Jeez. Charlie even talks like a banker! Where he got his formal speech patterns, I don't know. Maybe it's just that he reads so much . . . he even reads *Roget's Thesaurus* for fun.

It's wall-to-wall cranky people in every corridor and stairwell. At six p.m., everyone in Paris is streaming home from work. Charlie is still videoing away, after confiding to me that he's looking for particularly crabby expressions on "old fart frogs." This makes me laugh, maybe because it's the first thing out of his mouth this afternoon that's something a kid his age might say.

There are certainly lots of "old fart frogs" to choose

from. Some look stressed. Some look angry. Others just look tired. Every once in a while, someone shocks me by looking happy and thankful to be alive. I wonder, when I see these radiant faces, if they've found drugs or religion. I guess that's a terrible thing to say. Maybe they're just seduced by the essence of Paris.

Anyway, Charlie's having a ball, and I can't help but smile in the face of his innocence and delight in the simple pleasures of life—not to mention technology. It makes me feel a little lighter inside.

I propel Charlie onto a train on the 12 line, headed for Issy-les-Moulineaux, the suburb of Paris where we live now with Interpol agent Rebecca Morrow, her husband, and her daughter, Abby.

Evan, Charlie, and I are Rebecca's satellite kids. The three of us are enrolled in GI, but Abby isn't. Poor thing, she failed the basic recruitment tests—not that I think she cares all that much. Abby's mission in life is really just to fit in, be popular, and find a hot boyfriend. In short, she is totally normal, unlike the rest of us.

Abby is friendly; she's sweet . . . but there's something about the way she hurls herself at anyone "cool" that smacks of desperation. It's really off-putting. I always feel the urge to sit her down and explain this, but it would only hurt her feelings and make her even more socially desperate. Besides, it's not like I'm the poster child for popularity. These days, I could write a how-to manual on becoming an outcast.

As I ponder my role in GI, I get a weird, jumpy

feeling. A sensation that someone's watching me. It's nothing specific, just a gut thing. I look around but don't see anyone taking any notice of us.

I'm probably just sensitive to my little brother and his demented video-recording sunglasses, that's all. But he's not even gazing in my direction. He's now gone from studying people's faces to honing in on their shoes.

I shake my head. Don't be surprised if next year there's a big photography exhibit at the Centre Georges Pompidou or someplace, entitled: "Paris Metro: a la Chaussure! Photographs by Child Prodigy Charles Andrews."

I feel eyes drilling into my nape. I spin around, hoping to solve this mystery—and see a very normal business-woman dressed in a navy coat with a yellow scarf. I spin the other way and look straight into the face of Lisette Brun, one of Cecily Alarie's sidekicks.

Predictably, she makes a little *moue* with her pale, frosted lips and averts her gaze. I never "got" the word *"moue"* until I came to Paris. It's one of those terms that can only be demonstrated by a French chick, or maybe Kate Moss.

Next to Lisette, looking bored to tears, stands LuLu Something-or-Other, another GI snot and cohort of Cecily's. She spots me, lifts a dark eyebrow, and yawns before murmuring something into Lisette's ear. Something that I'm quite sure is about me and not complimentary, since they break into quiet laughter. Their gazes meet mine for another half second, then slide sideways toward the window, as if anything at all is more worthy of their attention than *moi*.

I'm really glad that ours is the next stop, and when the doors open with a whoosh, I tow Charlie off the train and into the noisy beehive that is the Metro station. Sounds assault our ears: the rumble of the trains, the galloping of thousands of shoes on concrete, the conversations and wails of children. The smells are overpowering too—wool and cologne, baking bread and coffee, body odor and a tinge of urine.

I'm glad when we're through the crowd, up the stairs, and out into the cool air of the street. Charlie has at last lost interest in his gizmo glasses and is dangling them by an earpiece. His feet are dragging, and I suspect he's experiencing a sugar low after all that cocoa and the pastry he inhaled.

"Here, let me take those." I put Matthis's precious video-shades into the outside zipper compartment on my backpack and grab Charlie's hand. "Almost home."

"It's not home," he says, looking forlorn. "We can never go home again."

That stops me in my tracks. I turn to face him and crouch down so that we're the same height. "Oh, Charlie. We'll make a new home one day. One that's just ours. I'm so sorry that all of this has happened."

"It's not your fault," he points out.

"I know . . . but . . ." I stare at his small, freckled button nose. It seems weighed down by the horn-rims, just as his innocence is weighed down by his extraordinary intelligence and appetite for knowledge. "I wish I could wave a magic wand and put everything back the way it was before."

He kicks at a cobblestone, then looks up and meets my gaze with old eyes, eyes that are wise beyond his years. "I don't. It wasn't that great, remember? Our parents were two big walking lies—we just didn't know it."

Rebecca Morrow's Paris town house on Rue Pierre Brossolette is tall and skinny. The living room, kitchen, and dining room are on the ground floor. Rebecca and Stefan, her husband, and Abby have bedrooms on the second floor. Charlie and I sleep on the third floor, while Evan has moved his things up into the small attic space, which is lit by a couple of decrepit dormer windows. He has to use a space heater because it's freezing up there, and in the summer he'll have to use an electric fan.

Evan could have stayed with us on the third floor, but this way everybody has a room and some privacy. And it would have been extremely weird to bunk right across the hall from him—it's weird enough to have him only one floor up.

The town house was built in the 1920s, so it's old-fashioned and smells . . . well, I'm not sure how to describe the smell, exactly. The scent of old wood and lemon furniture oil mingles with the smoke of almost a hundred years of fires in the hearth. The aromas of thousands of meals are trapped in the walls and ceilings; even fresh paint and wallpaper can't disguise it.

There's a musty, dusty odor from the oriental rugs, too—and the old paper and leather bindings of first edition books in Stefan's collection.

I use my key to unlock the front door. It's painted deep turquoise, same as the shutters. Nobody's hanging out in the living room or kitchen, so we troop up the stairs. Charlie keeps going up to the third floor, but I stop on the second to stick my head into Abby's room. "Hey, Abby-normal!" Charlie calls down the stairs, before I can even open my mouth.

She's got her earbuds in, and her head is bobbing to the music on her iPhone. She's painting her nails a pale mint green that looks gorgeous against her dark, olive skin. It would probably make me look yellow and ill.

"Hi, Abby," I say, loud enough that she hears me.

"Hey!" She finishes painting her pinkie nail, then screws the cap onto the polish and sets it down. She somehow jerks out the earbuds without messing up the polish.

"How was your day?"

"Awesome!"

There's a feverish glitter in Abby's eyes, an almost manic excitement. "You won't believe this . . . that girl LuLu, who hangs out with Cecily after class?"

"Yeah?"

"Well, she actually told me today that she likes my amethyst ring!"

I stare at her. So? The ring used to belong to Rita, and I'm the one who gave it to Abby because she loved it.

Abby gets off her bed and practically dances around

her room. I don't get it. Why is LuLu's compliment a cause for celebration?

"Don't you understand? She was *nice* to me, Kari! Actually nice."

"Great," I say cautiously. Alert the press . . . one of Cecily's sidekicks fell on her head and forgot to be bitchy.

Abby throws up her hands in exasperation. "I think she might want to be friends. With *me*."

"O-kaaay." I'm still not sure why this is so great.

"Hel-lo? An end to social Siberia? The dawn of a new age? These girls know hot guys!"

"Wait, I thought we were only talking about one girl?"

"LuLu is, like, Cecily's best friend. And Cecily— you're not going to believe this—asked me to grab her history book from school because she forgot it, so she's going to swing by here later." Abby is *glowing*. Because Roux used her for an errand. *Blek*.

And wait . . . Cecily asked Abby to bring home her gym bag, too, just last week. What kind of game is she playing?

But Abby is oblivious to my disgust.

"And we are all invited to Lisette Brun's opening at the end of the week," she continues, without a breath. "The one at her aunt's gallery, for her fashion illustrations? I did the flyers for her as a freebie, remember, because they'll look good in my design portfolio."

I nod and dredge up a smile for Abby, but I'm afraid that Lisette was only being polite, since Abby did the flyers for her. I hope for her sake that's not true, but I'm a realist. And I don't want to see Abby get hurt. "Cool," I manage. "What are you going to wear?"

I'm sidling toward the door. I just can't share her enthusiasm for hanging out with Mean Girls.

"I don't know," Abby wails in tones of agony. "What do you think I should wear?"

"Uh. Ask Cecily. You know I'm sort of hopeless at girl stuff, Abs. I can't even put on eyeliner or lipstick without looking like something Picasso painted during a bender."

But Abby has run to her closet and is flipping through the hangers as if her life depended on it.

"Yeah," I say. "So. I'll, um, see you at dinner, okay?"

"Okay . . ." Flip, moan, flip, sigh.

I flee up the stairs to my room, which I haven't bothered to decorate. The walls are white. No posters on them. There's a plain navy quilt thrown over the twin bed. Rebecca offered to buy me something more girlie, but I wasn't interested.

There's a simple, dark wood dresser that might or might not be an antique. On top are the few pictures I've brought with me: one of me and Kale in a karate competition, one of me and Rita, and one of me and Charlie. None of my parents.

It's been an insanely crappy day, and all I want is to hear a familiar voice from home. I flop on my bed, letting my hands and feet hang off the sides. I hear small footsteps clattering down the wooden stairs—Charlie's. I close my eyes and deliberately bring Luke's image to mind.

Luke, who kissed me like he meant it before Charlie and I got on the plane to Paris. Luke, who said he didn't care how many miles would be between us. Luke, who would never choke me unconscious in front of an entire classroom of people.

I sit up. I'm going to call him. I just need to hear his voice. I grab my phone and walk to the window as I scroll down my contact list. Outside, in the back-yard, I see Charlie on his knees in the frost-sprinkled dirt, collecting soil samples for some school science experiment.

I find Luke's name, highlight it, and hit the call but-ton as I turn away from the window. Miraculously, he answers on the second ring. "Hello?"

This is unheard of—we usually have to make appoint-ments in advance to talk, especially with the six-hour time difference.

"Hi, Luke. It's me." I check my watch—it's about noon in Washington, D.C.

"Kari! Hey . . . how are you?"

"Um. Good," I lie. "Just busy. You?"

"Same. I miss you."

"I miss you, too. . . ." There's a long, awkward pause. The thing is, Luke and I never really got a chance to hang out much before I left. We didn't really go on any dates. So we're together, but it's a bit weird.

"How's Rita? How's Lacey? Seen Kale at all?"

"Yeah—they're all good. Nothing really new."

"Oh." I stare at the floor and try to pick up a fallen pen with my toes. It doesn't work.

He clears his throat. "Listen, Kari. I should probably tell you something. . . ."

"What?"

"But I don't know how. I mean, I don't want you to get any ideas or get upset or anything—"

"Why?" I get a sick feeling in the pit of my stomach.

"Well . . ."

"Jeez, Luke, just say it already."

"Okay. Um, do you remember Tessa Wellington?"

"Of course. How could I not?" I ask drily. Tessa Wellington is gorgeous. She's a stunning brunette with long, natural corkscrew curls that cascade past her shoulder blades. She has huge blue-green eyes and the most perfect lips I've ever seen. But the worst thing about Tessa is that you can't even hate her, because she's nice. And funny. And . . . oh, God, why is Luke asking me if I remember her?

"Well, she kind of invited me to the winter formal. And since you're, uh, in Paris and all, I figured you wouldn't mind. So I said yes."

"You *what*?"

"I said yes."

I'm struggling to bend my mind around what he's telling me. Luke and Tessa? All dressed up, and dancing together, and maybe kissing each other in the heat of the moment? "You didn't think I'd *mind*?" My voice rises at least an octave.

"Kari, she didn't have a date, and I felt sorry for her."

"You felt *sorry*? For *Tessa*?" My voice is now yet another octave higher. "That's BS, Luke. Give me credit for some intelligence. Tessa is smoking hot. You may want to *do* her, but you definitely don't feel sorry for her!"

"Who said anything about doing anybody?" Luke's tone goes hostile. "We're just going to a freakin' dance."

"Right. You know, Luke, *we've* never gone to one together."

"When would we have? You're not here."

"That's not my fault!"

"Well, it's not mine, either. It's not like I asked you to move to Paris, Kari."

"It's not like anyone asked *me* if I wanted to move here!"

"Well, why are you there?"

"You know I can't talk about it."

Luke blows a raspberry into the phone. "Exactly. Because you'd have to kill me if you did, right? It's Top Secret. Frankly, Kari, I get enough of that from my dad, and I don't need it from my girlfriend, too. It gets really old."

"You're just going on the attack because you know you're in the wrong, Luke."

"I'm not attacking you, and I'm not in the wrong! I was only trying to be nice to the girl."

"Right. Just how nice are you planning to be?"

"I resent the implications of that."

"Yeah? Well, I resent the fact that you're going out with another girl, Luke. I thought you and I were *together.* As in, *exclusive.* As in, *not taking other people to formals*!"

"You're overreacting."

"I'm not! How would you feel if I told you I was going to some fancy thing with—with—" I search blindly for a name. "With Evan Kincaid?"

There's a long pause. When he finally answers, his tone is arctic. "You've always liked him. Wanna date him? Then go for it."

"I have not always liked him! I can't stand him. I just used his name as an example."

"Did you, now. Interesting. You know what, Kari, I'm tired of this conversation."

"Oh, my God. You don't *get* to be tired of the conversation—you started this fight! It's your fault."

"Yeah, whatever. I gotta go."

"You don't want to talk to me? Fine. You're tired of dating someone who lives in Paris? Fine. If you're so unhappy with me—and since you're going out with other girls anyway—then maybe we should just end it between us!"

And with that insanely stupid, emotional statement, I hang up on Luke.

Oh. My. God.

I didn't really mean to do it. It's like my brain watched in horror as my finger—without permission—punched the end button.

I broke up with Luke Carson.

And right before Christmas.

I am truly the most miserable person on the planet.

After this awful, beyond-sucky, catastrophic day, I can't even cry. Dry sobs emerge from my throat, but my tears have already been spent or fought off or . . . I don't know. I feel only a yawning emptiness.

I roll over on my bed and mash my face into the pillow. What idiot breaks up with Luke Carson?!

Me.

Chapter Four

Here's the thing—I can't even stay in my room for a big sulk or soul-searching session, because it's my turn to make dinner tonight. Agent Morrow doesn't cook, though she can probably kill a man with a pair of salad tongs.

Rebecca Morrow is one of the top dogs—if not THE top dog—at Interpol, so even if she can probably shoot an acorn off a sparrow's head at 800 yards, she's not the type to make muffins from scratch. And Stefan, her Greek linguistics professor husband, can translate a recipe from just about any language in the world but is pretty much barred from the kitchen for his own protection. He once injured himself while attempting to make coffee.

This means that Abby, Evan, and I rotate responsibility for grocery shopping, cooking, and laundry. We're all supposed to pitch in and clean, not that this happens with any regularity.

Tonight I'm supposed to make pasta with a white sauce and throw together a salad. I start with the salad because I'm in the mood to use a knife. I guillotine a head of lettuce and then rip the rest of it apart with my bare hands. . . .

As I'm rinsing some tomatoes and a cucumber, I glance through the window to the backyard and realize that Charlie's no longer out there. Maybe he's gone around to the front. I return to my gloomy thoughts and self-recriminations while I slice up the vegetables and toss everything into a bowl.

Then I wipe my hands on a dish towel and go to find my little brother. I haven't heard him come back into the house, and it shouldn't be taking him this long to get a few soil samples, even if the ground is hard and partially frozen. I open the front door and stick my head out, but there's no sign of him. "Charlie!" I call.

No answer.

"Chaaaarliiiiiie!"

Nothing.

Frowning, I trudge around to the left side of the house, then the right. But Charlie is nowhere in sight. In the backyard an ugly garden gnome strung with tinsel, a stone table, and two benches greet me. I yell for my brother yet again. Where could he have gone?

I circle around to the front yard and look down the street to see if he's talking with a neighbor or playing with someone's dog or cat. No Charlie.

At this point, I'm getting a little freaked out. My brother isn't the type to wander off alone—he's more likely to lose himself in a book or on an iPad. I cross the street to knock on Madame Pierre's door and ask in my lousy French if she's seen Charlie.

"Non," she says, shaking her gray-coiffed head. Have I looked around the corner, in the little park? He may be there playing on the swings.

After thanking her I go check, but he's not there, either.

Back at the town house, I ask Abby if she's seen Charlie. She hasn't. I go upstairs to our rooms, and even into Evan's room, yelling his name and peering under the beds in case he's playing some silly game—but instinct tells me he's not.

I pace back and forth in the kitchen. Where could Charlie have gone? A sick tide of fear washes over me. Has something happened to him?

Whom can I call? Agent Morrow is out of town for a few days. Stefan is in Greece. I reach for the house phone to call Evan, the only other person I can think of, but it rings before I can pick it up.

"Hello?"

"Karina Andrews?" The voice is heavily distorted, probably by some kind of machine. I can't tell if it's male, female, animal, or vegetable.

"Yes. Who's this?"

"We have your brother."

My heart stops. Then it turns over. Then it tries to gallop out of my chest.

"Karina?"

"Wh-why?" I whisper hoarsely. "Oh, my God. Don't hurt him!"

"Whether we hurt him or not," says the disembodied voice, "depends entirely upon you."

"On *me?*" My hand, the one clutching the receiver, drips sweat. I wrap my other one around it so that I won't drop the phone on the floor. As if from a long way away, I notice that my knees are shaking. Actually, it's my entire body. I struggle to hold the phone next to my ear.

"If you want to see your brother alive again, Karina, you will do exactly as we tell you."

I swallow, trying to drag some common sense up from the vortex of fear that's consuming me. "How do I know you really have him? How do I know he's alive?"

"Kaaaa-rrrriiiii!" Charlie shrieks into my ear. "Kaaari," he sobs. "Helllp! Come get me!"

Then I hear a smack and a howl.

"Stop it!" I scream. "Don't you dare hit him! I will *kill* you if you touch him again."

The voice on the phone laughs, and it's not a pleasant sound.

"I'll kill you!" My hands convulse around the hard plastic, and because it's slick with my sweat, the phone shoots up and out of my grasp, crashing to the floor. I panic and throw myself after it, scrabbling madly to get it once again to my ear. "Hello? Hello!"

"Get hold of yourself, Karina," the voice snaps. "Or it won't go well for your brother."

"Okay, okay . . . I am. I mean, what do you want?! You can't hurt him, *please*—"

"If you want to see Charlie alive again, you will do two things."

"*What?*"

"And you will not tell the authorities. You bring cops into this, Interpol, any type of law enforcement entity, and we will send you Charlie's head in a box."

Dear God, no. My stomach lurches, and I almost throw up just thinking about that image. Sweat pours down my face and back. I sag against the kitchen counter.

"Tell me what I have to do."

"You will go to a small town in Germany. There you will spring a young thief, Gustav Duvernay, from his confinement in a juvenile detention facility. Gustav will be familiar with the details of your next little project. You will work with him to see it to completion."

"What little project?"

"Stop asking questions and listen, Karina. You will have exactly one and a half weeks to accomplish your task. Your deadline is midnight on Day Ten. For every hour past midnight that you are late . . . you will receive a small gift from us: one of Charlie's fingers."

I can't help my swift, audible intake of breath.

"Do you understand?" the voice asks as I lean weakly on the sink.

"Yes," I manage.

"Good."

Then the caller gives me an address in Murnau am Staffelsee, Germany. He suggests that I arrive there by tomorrow evening. He suggests that "I bring my A game."

I have a suggestion for him too. But I am smart enough not to voice it. And to be honest, I'm too desperately afraid to make threats.

I'm tossing random clothes into my battered blue duffel when I hear the front door open and close, then Evan's footsteps on the stairs. Agent Morrow's are lighter, and she wears heels a lot. Evan takes the steps two at a time, with a heavy, masculine tread.

He stops on my floor and pokes his head into my room. "Hi."

"Hi," I say, my voice taut. My back is to him; my laptop is open on the bed; on the screen a message flashes that my e-mail has been sent.

"I'd ask how your day was, but . . ." He laughs ruefully.

"Worst. Day. Ever. Now, if you don't mind . . ."

"Bugger off?"

"Pretty much." I won't even look at him.

"Why are you packing?"

"Going on a trip."

"Where's Charlie?"

I don't answer.

"Kari?"

I toss a jacket, a climbing harness, and my set of lock picks into the duffel.

"Hey." He crosses the room, puts a hand on my shoulder, and forces me to face him, to look up into his level gray eyes. His perfect hair is dark with sweat—he's probably done an extra workout this evening. And a muscle jumps at his jaw. "What's going on?"

"Nothing." I jerk away and pull open a dresser drawer, tossing three pairs of socks into the bag.

"Damn it, Kari. Talk to me!"

But I'm hearing that horrible, distorted voice again in my mind. *You will not tell the authorities. You bring cops into this, Interpol, any type of law enforcement entity, and we will send you Charlie's head in a box.*

Pressing my lips together, I slam the sock drawer closed, then open the one containing jeans and toss two pairs of those into the duffel.

"Where's Charlie?" Evan asks me again, his eyes narrowing.

"I don't know." My voice breaks, to my shame.

"What do you mean, you don't know?" Evan's own voice is brittle.

"Someone has him. That's all I can tell you. Or they'll kill him."

Evan's eyes widen. "Who? How? Why?"

I shake my head. Then I open yet another drawer and throw a pair of black pants and a black turtleneck into the duffel, followed by a pair of black sneakers. "All I know is that one minute he was in the backyard, and the next he was gone. Then I got a phone call."

"They rang the house? We can trace it," Evan says. "I'll call Interpol." He pulls his cell phone out of his pocket.

"No!" I yell, knocking it out of his hand and jumping on it.

"Bloody hell, Kari." He stares down at me. I'm still hunched over on the floor, my body shaking. He crouches down and puts his big, warm hand on my back. "You're upset."

"No, really?" I shrug off his hand.

"Look, we'll call Rebecca. She'll know how to handle this."

"We *won't!*" My voice has become a scream.

Evan looks as if I've slapped him. "But—"

"They said they'd send me *his head in a box*. In a *box*, Evan. Oh, God . . ."

He sits down on the floor and pulls me onto his lap, into his arms. Tucking my head under his chin, he strokes my back and rocks me.

Is this really the guy who choked me out this morning? Humiliated me and dropped me to the floor?

Part of me wants to sob, but I can't—I'm too much in shock. Part of me wants to hug him back. But I also want to flatten him, because I don't have time for comfort. And he's not Luke . . . and even though I've broken up with Luke, it was accidental and this feels like cheating on him.

What is wrong with me? Why am I even thinking about stupid stuff like boys when Charlie has been kidnapped?! I struggle out of Evan's arms and stand up, even though he's still got hold of my hand.

"Hey," he says. "It's going to be all right. We'll find Charlie. I swear to you."

"There's no 'we' about this," I tell him. "I have to do this alone. They said no cops. No Interpol. No nothing. Or they will hurt my brother. Get it?"

"I'm not a cop. I'm not Interpol—" He breaks off as I snort.

"Last time I checked, GI stood for Generation Interpol, Evan! So I've probably endangered Charlie's life by talking to you. They're probably watching—"

"GI doesn't officially exist, Kari. They can't know about it. So they saw me come home. Big deal. They think we live as . . . as brother and sister."

I think about this for a moment. "But they must know Rebecca is Interpol."

He shrugs. "Maybe. So we won't call her. We'll handle this on our own. But I am with you on this. I won't let you go by yourself."

"You're not my boss, Evan. You have no way of stopping me." I toss a hairbrush and my toothbrush into the duffel bag and zip it closed with finality.

"Don't make me call the police, Kari," he says quietly.

"You'll get Charlie killed!" My voice rises on a note of hysteria.

"Then don't make me do it." Evan's face is like granite. Unyielding.

"You *asshole*. I can't believe you're threatening me."

He sighs. "It's only because I care. Not just about Charlie, but about you. Please, Kari. Let me help."

Can I risk it? Working with him? I don't have a lot of time to decide. It's yes or no. Life or death. I close my eyes and pray fervently that I'm making the right call. I open them and stare daggers at Evan. "Swear to me on the soul of your mother that you won't tell anyone, especially not Rebecca."

He nods. "I swear."

"Fine. Get packed. We're leaving in five minutes."

Evan sprints for the stairs. "Think about something while I get my things together. Consider telling your parents."

My mouth drops open. "Are you high? Are you nuts? Or are you just stupid?"

"No," he calls from the landing above.

"You're all three!" I follow him up to the attic while he rummages around and throws things into—what else?—a Prada weekender. Evan Kincaid is the only seventeen-year-old guy I know who'd own such a thing.

His room is nicely decorated, too, with black-and-white photographs that he's taken himself and a couple of framed art posters: Magritte and Picasso. The bedding is stark white and ridiculously expensive—I can't remember the name of the designer and don't care, but it's a Name. Evan's dresser is silver and black, and on top is a photo of his parents and a black leather box where he keeps watches and rings. The guy has more jewelry than I do, of course.

"Think about it, Kari."

"No. My parents are liars and traitors. They're despicable."

"Maybe. But they love Charlie—and they're very good at what they do."

"I will never speak to them again as long as I live."

"Fine. Don't. Send them an e-mail."

"That's traceable."

"Do it from an Internet café."

"I hate them!"

"Understandable. Yet you could use their help. So could Charlie."

I glare at Evan, who shrugs and continues his packing. "They're not the authorities," he says in a mild tone.

I don't reply.

"Kari?"

"Drop it, Evan! I wouldn't even know how to get in touch with them if I wanted to, and I don't."

Evan walks over and puts his hand on my shoulder again. The heat of it burns through my thin sweater. "Remember the envelope taped to the back of the painting you burned?"

I hesitate, then nod. I set a family portrait on fire after I found out about my parents. There was some kind of letter attached to it, but I refused to even look at it. Evan pulled it from the flames before it got destroyed.

"Well, it contained information on how to get a message to them."

"I don't care," I say, moving away from his touch. "They're dead to me."

Evan sighs, then changes the subject. "So where exactly are we going, Kari? And what are we going to do once we get there?"

Chapter Five

I fill Evan in about our new buddy, the thief. Gustav Duvernay is being held at a juvenile detention center in Murnau am Staffelsee. While it's probably not a maximum security facility, it will definitely be guarded and no cakewalk to get into. We certainly won't be able to waltz in after signing up for a guided tour.

We're going to need some help, and Evan convinces me that it's not practical to run out the door within five minutes. We'll need to take a train in the morning.

Since I refuse to even consider contacting my parents, we decide to call Matthis. He's brilliant, resourceful, and capable of keeping his mouth shut.

Matthis arrives within a half hour, looking rumpled and almost as stressed as I am. Charlie is really his only friend, and he's beyond worried.

In the meantime, after a huge debate with myself

about the risk, I have called Kale on Rebecca's secure line and told him to ditch class, then find a way of getting Rita out of Kennedy Prep for the afternoon. We may need them both in order to break out this Gustav person—Kale for his muscle and knowledge of martial arts, and Rita because she has hacking skills that Matthis may not.

I have Matthis do a sweep for monitoring software, then install an encryption program for messages and files on all our cell phones. He also puts extra security on all our laptops. We comb the Internet for information on Duvernay, and find that he is a world-class cat burglar. Then I hold my breath and pray that I haven't made a huge mistake as Rita and Kale Skype in from his apartment in Washington, DC.

"Hey, Kari." Kale looks the same as always, compact and muscular with his black hair short and razor cut, his handsome Japanese features set in calm lines. The only indication that he's worried is in his left fist. He keeps clamping it around his thumb, then releasing it and doing it again.

Rita sits down next to him on his bed, which is covered in a pale blue spread. Behind them is a landscape of ducks flying low over a river. She waves, somberly. The usual spiky ponytail rides high on her head, and she's got on dark green Calvin Klein glasses that match her sweater. Rita's got an entire wardrobe of the coolest designer frames, all made to order in her prescription.

"Hey," I say, knowing I don't look anywhere near calm.

"You remember Evan, right? And this is Matthis, a friend from the Paris Institute. He's Charlie's buddy."

"Hi, Matthis," Kale says. He turns back to me. "So who are these people who have Charlie?"

"We don't know. I couldn't even tell if the caller was male or female."

Rita asks, "What do they want you to do for them?"

"Break a thief out of custody. Then steal something with him."

The two of them exchange a glance. "Steal what?"

"I don't know."

Their eyebrows shoot up in tandem. "Huh?"

"They haven't told Kari what it is yet," Evan explains. "But the thief has a rap sheet for art and jewel heists, so it's probably something like that."

"Oh, that's all," Rita says, as if we're going to be snatching a pack of gum from a 7-Eleven convenience store. "Awesome."

Kale runs his tongue along his front teeth. Gives one quick nod. "So how can we help?"

"Well, we need some of Rita's talent, first of all," I say.

Evan gets more specific. "Hack into this juvenile detention center's computer system. Find the files on Duvernay, Gustav. Report anything useful that will help us break him out."

"Spell the name?" Rita grabs a pen off Kale's corner desk.

I do. I also spell the name of the detention center.

"Just a thought," says Kale. "Why not get into the facility by pretending that one of you is in police custody and checking in as a prisoner?"

"That's a good idea," I concede. "Rita, can you find out the protocol or process?"

"Yes. Give me a few hours. I'll get you everything I can find."

"Thanks." I hesitate. "I, um . . . I know I don't really have the right to ask, after I got us into so much trouble. But I—"

"Don't be ridiculous," Rita says. "This is Charlie's life we're talking about!"

I look down at the floor. Then back up at her screen image. "Yeah."

"You okay?" Kale asks.

"Peachy. Homicidal, but other than that, great."

Evan breaks in. "Right. The three of us—Kari, me, and Matthis—will book tickets on the train from Paris to Munich. We'll ring you back to see what you find."

"Yup," Kale says. "When?"

"Exactly twelve hours from now," I tell him.

"That's, like, four a.m. here," Rita points out.

I nod. "Sorry. We have less than ten days to get everything done."

"It's just hard to get around my parents." She yanks on her ponytail, thinking. "But they should be comatose at four a.m., so I should be able to sneak onto the desktop computer in my dad's home office."

"Can you pretend you're spending the night with—"

She shakes her head. "Not on a school night. No way."

"I'll get to your house," Kale says. "Can you let me in without waking your parents?"

"Yeah, I think so. Come to the back door, off the

kitchen, okay? Kari, we'll figure it out. We'll Skype you at four a.m.—if all goes well."

"Cool," I say. "Thanks. I really miss you both."

"Same," Kale says. "Stay calm."

I blow out a breath. "Easy for you to say."

He nods in compassion.

"Bye, Kari." Rita blows me a kiss. "Hang in there."

Just as Evan, Matthis, and I are logging out of Skype, the doorbell rings.

My heart stops.

Matthis, always jumpy, squeaks and rears back, almost smacking the lenses of his metallic blue glasses with his kneecaps.

Evan's eyebrows shoot up to his hairline, and he grins.

"Spaz," I mutter.

Matthis takes a deep breath and settles himself onto Evan's rug. He reminds me of a praying mantis.

"Who would come to the door this late?" I ask. "It's after ten p.m."

Evan shrugs. "I'll get it."

Fear is having its way with me again. "Oh, God. Evan, what if somehow the kidnappers know that I've told people about Charlie, and they've sent me one of his fingers?!"

He takes me by the shoulders. "You haven't left the house. There are no cops here. Why would they do that?" But he grabs a gun out of his desk drawer, rams home the clip on his way downstairs, and tells us to stay upstairs.

I feel sick, but I follow on Evan's heels, disregarding his order to stay put. He gives me a dirty look, which I meet with my best impression of an impassive stare.

Evan puts his eye to the keyhole, frowns, and shoves the gun into his waistband. He turns the deadbolt and throws open the door. I'm ready for anything—anything except Cecily Alarie, of all people. I'd totally forgotten that she was coming to get her history book from Abby.

She comes strutting in. "*Bonsoir,* Evan," she says to him with a dazzling smile. She kisses him on each cheek. For me, no kisses. She has only a tiny, disapproving sniff. "Kari." *Kahrrrhi.*

"Cecily. This is quite a surprise," I say. "What brings you to the unfashionable burbs in the dead of night?" But I know exactly why. She wants to see Evan. That's why she's "forgetting" things at school—it's so transparent.

"Abby has my heestory book. And besides, she called to ask for my assistance," Cecily says airily. "It eez a fashion emergency."

A fashion emergency. Right.

"We must find her a dress for Lisette's art opening on Friday. You are coming, yes, Evan?"

"Uh . . ." He stalls.

Cecily sidles up to him and lays her hand on his arm. "Lisette would be so touched if you did." No man could resist those curves; that accent. *Ugh.*

"Well . . ." Evan casts about for something to say, just as Abby clatters down the stairs in a pair of high heels. I'd break my neck if I tried to negotiate steps in those.

"Cecily!" She looks like a kid on Christmas morning. "Ohhh! I cannot thank you enough for coming over to guide me!"

Gack. Any more effervescence and she'll foam over like a bottle of soda after it's been shaken.

Cecily beams at her and runs over to kiss both of her cheeks too. "I am 'appy to 'elp."

Since when?

She casts a sidelong glance at Evan as she moves toward the stairs, to see if he's checking her out.

Ugh.

My only consolation is that he doesn't pay much attention to her as she undulates up the stairs like Sofia Vergara in her clingy hot pants and formfitting sweater.

Cecily aces things in deportment class (my second least favorite, after Tech 101) like the Model Strut she just demonstrated. She's also a whiz at gracefully getting out of a taxi—with perfect posture, knees together.

And me? The last time I got out of a taxi, I accidentally flashed my underwear to a whole sidewalk full of people.

I'm close to failing deportment. I'm not even sure how that's possible, given how stupid it is, but I am. Madame Blumenthal despairs that I will ever be able to hold a teacup or a champagne glass properly. And evidently I "swig" rather than "sip" my beverages. I "chomp" rather than "delicately savor." Yeah, what*ever.*

Cecily and Abby start chattering like a couple of squirrels and disappear into Abby's room. As soon as her door closes, Matthis slinks down the stairs and shrugs into his jacket. "Meet you at the train station tomorrow morning," he mumbles.

"Matthis, what will you tell your mom and dad?"

He chews on his lip and shoves his glasses higher on

his nose. "Huh. Hadn't even thought about it."

"You'll need some kind of cover story if you're going to disappear to Germany for days," Evan tells him.

"Special GI field course?" Matthis suggests.

I shake my head. "Too easy for them to check with the program."

He chews on his lip some more. "Got it. A special chess competition. I made the finals, which are being held in Munich."

"Will they believe that?" Evan asks.

Matthis nods. "I've never lied to them before." His expression is a little guilty.

"Yeah, you're not the juvenile delinquent type," Evan teases him. "Unlike me." He adds this with a wink.

"How are you going to explain being gone?" I ask Evan.

"I actually have been on special field assignments for Rebecca," he says. "So that'll work. You, though? You'd better call in sick with a really nasty flu."

"But Abby will know the truth," I point out.

He frowns. "We'll have to swear her to secrecy."

Matthis disappears into the chilly December night, which leaves me standing alone with Evan in the hallway.

"You okay?" he asks softly.

No. I'm not okay at all, but I need to be, for Charlie's sake. I have to be strong for him, and smart for him. My mind flashes back to the sound of the smack I heard over the phone, and I cringe. I hope to God they only did that to get a reaction from me. I begin to pray silently.

Please let them not be beating him on a regular basis. Please let them be feeding him and keeping him comfortable. I

hope he's not terrified . . . dear God, he's only seven years old.
Please keep him safe. Please. I will do anything—just please,
keep him safe until I can get him away from those monsters.

"Kari?" Evan prompts.

"I'm . . . fine." I shove my hands into my pockets as I
remember the feeling of being in his arms, sitting in his
lap, my head tucked under his chin. Awkward.

He's gazing at me with an enigmatic expression. I have
no idea what he's thinking.

"Listen, Evan . . . thank you."

"For forcing my way into this operation?" he asks drily.

"For helping. For being a friend."

Evan takes two quick steps toward me, and suddenly
I'm back in his arms. It feels way too good. My cheek feels
way too comfortable resting over his heart, the rhythm of
which is way too strong, steady, and reassuring.

"We'll get Charlie back. I promise you, Kari. Okay?"

"Okay," I whisper.

He starts to say something else, but a feminine throat
clears audibly right above us.

Evan breaks away from me, and I feel momentarily
lost—how ridiculous.

Cecily is lurking on the first-floor landing, Abby behind
her. Cecily lets her mask slip for a moment, looking as if
she just sucked on a lemon. Then she regains her poise.

"Oh, Evan—we need a man's opinion," she purrs.
Ehvahn. Gag.

I have to control my urge to deck her.

"An opinion on what?" he asks, his voice light. He
heads for the stairs, taking them two at a time, as usual.

"On a dress . . ." Her voice fades as they both head to Abby's room.

I stay by myself downstairs, in the dark living room. Clearly they do not want *my* input, and I'm feeling really screwed up, on so many levels . . . confused about Evan, freaked about Charlie, mad at Luke, still sick about my parents.

Exhausted, I eventually fall asleep on the couch for a fitful couple of hours. I have nightmares about Charlie. Is my little brother okay?

Chapter Six

The next morning I stand with Evan and Matthis on a platform at the Gare de l'Est waiting for our train to Stuttgart. Besides the two hours on the couch, I haven't slept, due to nightmares about Charlie being mistreated. I'm so afraid for him.

Have they tied him up? Drugged him? Is he chained to a radiator? Using a bucket for a toilet? Are they feeding him? I deliberately blank my mind to anything worse—I can't take it. I'll get hysterical and then I'll be useless to my brother.

It's very cold, and the holiday decorations everywhere seem to mock me. My attitude is growing worse, if that's possible. I can't even remember the person I was before my parents turned traitor and took off . . . that girl seems so young, so naive, and so long ago.

I scan the crowd around us, for lack of anything better to do. There's an elderly man reading an Arabic newspaper, his lips moving ever so slightly. A matronly woman talks on a cell phone. And a couple in their midthirties holding hands, but with an odd lack of intimacy. Almost as if they're doing it for show.

Something about them looks vaguely familiar, but I can't place them. I nudge Evan and cut my eyes toward them. He scans them discreetly but shakes his head.

Matthis can't stand still. He puts on his own pair of video sunglasses. He alternately taps one foot, then the other. He fishes through his pockets for something. He paces. He rubs at his neck. Looks around.

Evan keeps up a patter of deliberately polite, cheerful conversation that is meant to distract and relax me, but instead sets my teeth on edge. I want to tell him to please be quiet, but I know he's only trying to be kind.

I'm not sure I deserve kindness. After all, I'm the one who let Charlie go outside by himself. Paris is a big city. He was alone and vulnerable. If I'd just stayed with him, the kidnappers might not have him now.

I'm still beating myself up when the train pulls alongside the platform and it's time to board. The three of us find a compartment with no one in it and take seats, Evan and I across from each other and Matthis next to me with his feet propped up on the opposite seat. He immediately puts away the sunglasses, pulls out his iPad, and fades into his own high-tech fantasy world. He still fidgets, though. I wonder if Matthis is ADHD, or if he's always this high-strung.

Evan leans back and smiles, as if we're all going off on some holiday.

Me? I brood and obsess and fight off more images of Charlie being mistreated. I hope Rita is having lots of success hacking into the system at the juvie facility. I want to know every possible detail of what goes down there.

Evan tries to lure me into a discussion about French politics, but my eyes glaze over and he eventually gives up. He puts in his earbuds and listens to music.

I fold my arms across my chest, close my eyes, and pretend to sleep, but what I really do is brood for the next three-odd hours, the scenery outside blurring as the train rumbles along. Finally I'm driven from the car by the need to pee, so I exit and go to find the WC.

When I step out again, the woman who was holding hands with the man on the platform is standing near the door. I hold it open for her, since it's the polite thing to do. She smiles and nods her thanks.

When I turn my back on her, I notice her companion ahead of me, blocking my path. The woman jabs me in the kidneys with something hard—the barrel of a gun? Then she leans forward and whispers into my ear. "This is an H and K semiautomatic. It will easily blow out your small intestines. Walk very slowly. Don't try anything—I won't hesitate to shoot. Turn right into the empty car just ahead. Then sit down."

I process my shock and her orders. First Charlie, now me?

What is going on? Who is targeting us?

I could drive my elbow backward, into her gut, and then try to get her in a choke hold, but it's risky—not only to myself but to other passengers on the train. If it were just her I had to contend with, I might try it, but the man she's with also has his hand around something in his pocket, probably another gun.

I have no option but to do as she says. I move forward and then enter the car. It smells like stale cigarettes and spilled coffee.

"Sit!" the man says, flanking me.

I do. "What do you want?"

He ignores me. So does she. They avoid meeting my eyes.

I try again. "Who are you? Why are you doing this? What's this about?"

No answer.

"Who do you work for?"

They stare at me, faces impassive.

Wonderful.

I have a brief surge of hope as a porter appears, his eyebrows raised. He gestures at me. "You find her, eh, your runaway daughter?"

The woman produces an effusive, grateful smile. "Oh, yes, thank you—"

I open my mouth to scream, "Help!" But the man sends a ferocious warning look my way, and I realize that they won't hesitate to shoot the porter. He probably has a wife and kids . . . again, I don't want to risk it. I can somehow get away from these two later. I know I can.

The man says gruffly to the porter, "Please—you will alert us if her no-good boyfriend or the idiot friend come this way? We would rather avoid an ugly scene."

"Of course, Monsieur. *Tout de suite.*" He shoots me a disapproving glance.

Thanks, pal. Really, you couldn't be more helpful. Couldn't you ask for ID, at least? How do you know these two aren't planning to kidnap me into sex slavery?

But I don't say a word. I just hunch my shoulders and glare sullenly at all of them.

The porter whistles a tune as he walks away.

I assess the people who are holding me captive. The woman is brunette and wears an ugly printed scarf. She has dressed in a deliberately dowdy, gray sack dress and black tights, but under them she is lean and fit. I'd say she's a runner, which is bad news for me. She's got on serviceable shoes with rubber soles.

The man has closely cropped dishwater-blond hair, graying beard stubble, and pale eyes that are devoid of expression. The two of them seem neither intelligent nor stupid; just well trained to carry out someone's orders.

I wonder about that someone—and try asking again.

Sack-Dress Woman tells me curtly to shut up.

Does the person they work for have Charlie?

I don't think so. It doesn't make sense that the kidnappers would demand that I spring this Gustav guy but then snatch me off a train en route to do that. Unless it was a ruse? But that doesn't add up either . . . they could have grabbed me off a street in Paris.

So who are Sack-Dress and Beard-Stubble? And who's calling the shots?

The train slows as we pull into Karlsruhe, the last stop

before Stuttgart, where we have to transfer to another train for Munich.

I wonder if Evan has fallen asleep—he certainly hasn't come looking for me, and I've now been gone at least twenty minutes.

Sack-Dress grabs my arm and hauls me to my feet before propelling me out of the car, into a line of departing passengers, and then down the steps to the platform. Beard-Stubble is right behind me. I pretend to trip and fall—he grabs me and pulls me upright.

There's a family of four waiting to board—two little boys and their parents. I reach back while Stubble is distracted and lift the flap of his coat so that the gun in his pocket is clearly visible.

One of the little boys points. "Papa! That man has a gun!"

"A gun?" repeats his brother loudly.

"Gun!" screams the mother. She grabs her sons and hits the pavement, while her husband crouches protectively over them.

Chaos erupts in the busy train station. People run screaming; a couple of German cops in khaki uniforms come running.

I take full advantage, kicking Stubble in the balls and twisting out of Sack-Dress's grip. I sprint back to the train, which is about to pull out of the station.

But she's got quick reflexes. She comes back after me, as Stubble rolls on the ground clutching himself.

I kick out and slam her in the chest, but she recovers and drops back to the next entrance. She makes it onto the train at the same time I do, just on the opposite end of the car, which is deserted since a big group of people just got off.

Great.

I cannot give her time to pull that gun and aim it at me.

So I rush her like a small linebacker, then aim a round-house kick at her face. She dodges it, but it throws her off-balance. I aim another kick between her shoulder blades, and she goes facedown into the aisle. *Lick the floor and like it, lady.*

I hurdle over her and erupt through the doors of the car, slamming into a startled porter.

"Hey!" He goes head over heels.

As he rights himself, brushing off his pants, Sack-Dress knocks him flying again.

"Herr Gott!" He follows this with a series of curses.

I just keep running—until Sack-Dress body-slams me into the floor before I get to the doors of the next car. My turn to eat dirt.

Where is Evan when I need him? Or Matthis, who could at least stick out a foot and trip this woman? They can't be more than two cars away—if that.

"Kincaid!" I shriek. "Help!"

Her knee is in the small of my back, and she's got me by the hair. I buck with all my might, ignoring the pain and the ripping sound. I dislodge her enough to roll onto my side, then chop the heel of my hand into her windpipe.

She falls back, clutches at it, and makes a gurgling noise.

Then, and only then, does Evan pop up out of nowhere.

There's a waft of elegant aftershave, a blur of French blue poplin shirt, and then presto! Evan's sitting astride her, her face is squashed into the floor, and he's zip-tying her hands behind her back.

Zip ties? I lift an eyebrow. Really?

I scrape myself up and out of the aisle. I tear my gaze from his buns—hey, it was impossible not to notice them—and drop into a seat, panting. "Where did you get those?"

He turns his head, evaluates me in one laser-swift glance, then gives me a sweet, devastating smile. "The zip ties? They're never missing from the Kinky Aid Kit. Didn't you know?"

"The *what*?"

Matthis appears, his eyes wide and solemn behind the blue metallic frames of his glasses.

"Kincaid. Kinky Aid. Ha, ha. Get it?"

I close my eyes. "Seriously?"

When I open them again, Evan's grin has widened.

"Are you okay?" Matthis ventures.

But I'm staring, furious, at what's still clutched in Sack-Dress's right fist. "Oh. My. God." I put a hand to my hair, which feels all wrong. And my scalp is throbbing.

Evan winces, pries open the woman's fingers, and removes a torn hank of my hair. "Ummm." He extends it to me. "D'you want it back?"

I gape.

Matthis chokes.

The twice-flattened porter appears. "Are you all right?" He glances dubiously at my hair.

I do not even want to know what it looks like. . . .

"Ah. Uh," mumbles Matthis. "I'm gonna suggest . . . maybe . . . a weave. You know, temporarily."

This can't be good.

I don't have a lot of time to worry about it, though, because Evan gets off Sack-Dress and hauls her to her feet. I'm pleased to see that she doesn't look so good, either. Her nose is broken and gushing blood. She's got a black eye. She's pretty banged up—and it's not as if *her* hair is Oscar-worthy, either. It's not pretty, but at least it's not half ripped out.

Evan keeps a firm grip on her with one hand and pulls out his GI badge with the other. He shows it to the porter.

"Evan Kincaid. Junior officer with Interpol. We were simply going on holiday. This woman tried to kidnap and attack my friend here. Can you call a couple of other porters and take her into custody?"

Sack-Dress tries to break away from Evan, but he knocks her feet out from under her, gentleman that he is. At least he holds her upright—if it were up to me, I'd let her fall back onto her face.

The porter gets on his walkie-talkie thing. Within minutes, three other porters come running, and they hustle us all into a special first-class car, though they seem suspicious of Evan's GI credentials. One of them gets a first aid kit. They clean Sack-Dress's face and pack her nose, telling her to lean her head back. She refuses to look at me. Her hands are shaking.

I'm thinking this is weird, except I look at my own hands and they're just as bad. I guess it's adrenaline. A different porter squats down next to me and tries to clean my face, but I tell him it's not necessary and wave him away.

"Trust me, it's necessary," says Evan. He takes over. How is it that Evan has not a hair out of place and still smells like royalty? His aftershave must cost a thousand dollars an ounce.

He bites his lip as he takes my chin in his hand. I try to jerk away from him but find that I can't. "Keep still," he orders. Then, as if I'm three years old, he wipes my mouth. Really, the last time anyone did this, I was wearing pull-ups.

"Well," he says, "you won't need a collagen injection for a while."

Huh?

He turns my head to inspect my hair and grins. "Matthis? About that weave you mentioned . . ."

"I don't care what my hair looks like!" I say. "I only care about Charlie."

"Okay," Evan says, but he looks amused. "But you'll need a hat or a wig."

I guess I should probably look at the back of my head. "Give me a mirror, then."

Everyone—all the porters, Matthis, and Evan—exchanges a glance.

"Right," Evan says. "Get the girl to a mirror."

The first porter points to a door right outside the car.

I get up and walk toward it, not without a feeling of dread. I'm no girlie girl, but everyone has a *little* vanity.

It's very cramped inside the WC, and the light isn't

great. But there's enough for me to see that my mouth is swollen to the size of an inner tube. There are cuts and abrasions on my face, which despite Evan's attempts, is still not clean.

I gingerly try to angle my head so that I can see the back of it, but my brain feels like its sloshing inside my skull. Then there's a shout and a scuffle outside. A thump. A slam. Another shout.

I throw open the door just in time to see Sack-Dress hurl herself bodily off the train. Understand that I'm no fan of hers . . . but even I wince, horrified, as she bounces down the embankment and rolls toward the river we're passing. Oh, my God! Her hands are still behind her back, zip-tied.

That doesn't change as she hits the water like a sack of cement and sinks.

I don't even realize it, but I'm screaming.

The porters are shouting too, and one of them gets on his comm unit to alert the engineer, but the train shows no signs of braking.

Evan hauls me away from the still-open door and back into the car. "It's okay, it's okay, it's okay, Kari," he repeats.

"It's not okay! They have to stop the train—someone's got to pull her out of the water!"

"They can't stop the train easily. Even if they did, by the time someone got to her it would be too late. And there may be other trains coming behind us on the same set of tracks."

"But—but—"

"I'm sure the engineer has alerted the German police."

He settles me onto a bench and rubs my arms.

"She's going to drown!"

"Yes." His gray-blue eyes are somber. I know he's thinking about the fact that he put the zip ties on her wrists.

"She committed suicide." I say it baldly.

He drags a hand over his face, then nods.

"Who is she? Why did she target me? Is she trying to bring me to whoever has Charlie? No—that doesn't make sense. So there's *another* person after us?"

Evan just looks at me. "I don't know."

"And why did she kill herself? *Why?*"

He shakes his head. "To some people, some organizations, failure is not an option. And she failed to bring you to whoever ordered your kidnapping. Maybe death is preferable to the consequences that await her. "

I think about that. About failure not being an option.

And I realize that it's true for me as well. No matter what happens, no matter who tries to stop me, I will break Gustav Duvernay out . . . because failing Charlie isn't an option. It's unthinkable.

Chapter Seven

There is a lot of confusion onboard the train, need-less to say. And off the train, once we get to Stuttgart. The first porter, the one who thought I was a runaway daughter, cannot seem to understand that I was actually being kidnapped by strangers.

"Your *maman*—she is the one who threw herself into the river?" he asks stupidly.

"She's *not* my mother!" I say, for what seems like the tenth time.

"But regardless of who she is, you should send the *polizei* to pull her body out of the water," Evan points out.

"Yes, yes, of course." He mops at his brow with a handkerchief. Despite the chilly weather, he's sweating profusely. "They have been dispatched."

"You should have asked for the woman's ID—and

his—before leaving me alone with those people," I tell the porter.

"But you were already with them . . . I saw no need . . . you didn't ask for help—" He flounders helplessly. Dark, wet circles are growing under the arms of his uniform.

"I didn't ask for help because they had a gun jammed into my ribs." My tone is pure acid.

"So you are a minor?" Another porter asks this question and demands to see our passports. "You are all minors?"

It goes on and on, the confusion.

Evan calls Interpol. To my surprise, he asks for someone I've never heard of instead of Rebecca; he speaks a language that I can't even begin to interpret. It's not French, not German. Perhaps it's Dutch? Where did he learn that? I have no idea. But evidently the porters don't speak it either, because they continue to scratch their butts and give us a hard time. Evan gives a sequence of numbers—a code?—to the person on the other end of the line and then ends the conversation.

"What were those numbers?" I ask in low tones.

"Code for 'training mission.' That will reassure them that there's nothing going on."

"Oh."

At last the Person On High In Charge of Porters calls them and strikes the fear of God into them, and we are taken to a German Interpol office of some kind. We're shoved into an office suite there, where a kindly older gentleman seems amused at the sight of my hair. I'm finally inspired to go and look at it again—which is a big mistake.

I twist, turn, and contort to check out the full extent of the damage in the Interpol office's bathroom mirror. Most of my hair is one length and streams past my shoulder blades. Then there's the large hank of it that's ripped jaggedly across and only about six inches long. Nice. I can only imagine how hard Cecily Alarie would laugh if she could see this.

I'll need some hair extensions—or at the least a wig or a hat. Oh, well. Frankly, I'm a lot more worried about Charlie than I am about my hair. And I guess it could be worse: The woman could have ripped it completely out.

Honestly, my face looks worse than my hair. I'm not sure what we can do about *it*—just smear it with makeup, I guess. And like I said, I don't care.

"Kari?" Evan's voice calls through the door.

"What?" Despite the fact that I have bigger worries, I'm not happy he's seen me looking like this. But it's better than Luke seeing me this way. Right?

"I think it may be possible to French-braid your hair so that it covers the part that's—" He hesitates.

"Missing?"

There's a weird snorting sound.

"Are you *laughing?*" I fling open the door. He's doubled over, nose pinched, gasping for air in between chortles.

My mouth works.

Matthis makes himself small.

I lunge at Evan and pound my fists into him—any part I can reach.

"Ow! Damn it, Kari—"

"You. Do. Not. Get. To. Laugh." I keep pummeling him. Maybe my reaction is out of proportion, but I have a lot of leftover adrenaline from that fight. "Not. Funny!"

He laughs so hard that tears run down his face. "Yes it is . . . oooof . . . sorry . . . but it is!" He finally twists and captures my wrists and forces me back against the wall.

That makes me so mad that I think about spitting in his face.

"Don't," he warns.

Boy, do I want to work up a good loogie. It would look awesome right in the middle of his forehead.

"Don't," he says again.

"Let go of me."

He shakes his head. "I'm restraining you for my own good." He stares down at me for a long moment. "Besides, you're not the ugliest girl I've ever had against a wall."

I'm speechless.

He grins provocatively. "In fact, you're rather hot."

This gives me a perverse thrill that I'm instantly ashamed of. And I *so* do not know how to respond. So I take refuge in arguing with him.

"I'm *not* hot. My hair is torn and my lips look like they got stuck in a vacuum cleaner and *none* of this has anything to do with finding Charlie, so—"

Evan brushes his lips over my swollen ones.

Wait, did he just do that?

Then he releases my hands and turns away.

I almost slide down the wall.

Suddenly the door to the suite opens and a no-nonsense gray-haired guy in a suit walks in, looking down at a file and then up at us. "Andrews, Karina? Kincaid, Evan? Matthis, Clearance?"

"Yes." Evan speaks for us all.

Which is good, because I still don't think I can.

"You can go," the German man says without further explanation or introduction. He pulls our passports from the file and hands them to us after a quick perusal of each. "Interpol vouches for you." He frowns down at the file once more. "However, Mr. Matthis is to check in regularly with his parents on his progress during the, ah, chess tournament." The blandness in his voice is commendable.

Matthis blushes, of course. Pushes up his glasses. Fidgets.

Gray-Hair continues. "And Ms. Andrews, you should drink plenty of fluids and have some chicken soup for dinner. To aid in your recovery from the flu, of course."

I clear my throat.

"I'll make sure she does that," Evan says with an easy smile.

"Very good."

Matthis glances at me, then Evan, as if to say, *can we get out of here now?*

"Well, then," says Gray-Hair. "How delightful to have met the three of you, despite the circumstances."

"Oh, no," Evan assures him. "The pleasure's been all ours."

And with that whopper, we're ushered to the door and into a waiting taxi.

We ask to be taken the short distance back to the Stuttgart train station, and from there we resume our trip to Munich. We pray that we don't encounter any more mystery attackers—or Interpol again, especially given our odd agenda.

Next stop: disguises. Munich is a big city, a great city for a disappearing act. I don't know what I expected of Munich, but it wasn't beauty, grace, and charm. Evan has the cab take us to a small, quiet hotel off the beaten path that's only a few minutes' walk to the city center at Marienplatz.

Despite my increasing anxiety about Charlie's well-being, I can't help but notice the stunning, soaring neo-Gothic city hall—and I can't reconcile the appearance of this building with its name, the Rathaus. It just doesn't sound right.

While we don't have either the time or the inclination to sightsee, I make a mental note that someday, I'd like to come back here.

Evan seems to read my thoughts. "Lovely, isn't it? A pity we can't stop in at the Alte Pinakothek or the Residenz or the Schloss Nymphenburg."

I shrug.

"You'll have to return in summer," Evan adds, "and go to the English Garden. It's breathtaking, and you'll find surfers at the rapids in the river. Though you may stumble across the odd naked person sunning himself on the grass, which is a bit alarming."

I give him an incredulous look, and he shrugs. "Most Germans think nothing of it."

I'm trying to imagine a bunch of nudists on the mall in Washington, DC, as Evan leads us into the Augustiner Bräu, the oldest brewery in Munich. In the States, there's no way they'd let us in, but in Europe the drinking age for wine and beer is sixteen.

We don't order anything but food and coffee, though. We're not here to party. We're here to steal—excuse me, *borrow*—a car and get out of Dodge.

We sit on benches at long, low, rough-hewn wooden tables. Over a lunch of sauerbraten, sausages, and some much-needed hot soup, we take stock of our surroundings. Unfortunately for our cash flow, this is a pretty upscale area, full of galleries, jewelry stores, and boutiques.

Evan shakes his head. We won't be able to find what he has in mind here . . . or will we? Over our protests, he leaves Matthis and me to our café au laits and disappears for about half an hour. When he returns, he's carrying an old mesh shopping bag with a wad of clothing inside. And an oversize artist's portfolio.

"What's that?" I ask.

"You'll see. Come on. Let's change and then find the nearest American hotel."

Evan drags us—yes, even me, though I protest— into the men's WC. There are separate locking stalls (without gaps at the top or bottom like US bathroom stalls). Since someone has clearly targeted me and knows who I'm traveling with, it's time to change my appearance.

Evan pulls his strange wad of clothing out of the shopping bag and starts to distribute it.

"Where did you get this stuff?" I ask.

"I broke into a small house nearby and raided the closets," Evan says in a nonchalant tone.

Why am I not surprised? "Of course you did."

Matthis gets a simple, dark blue cap embroidered with the logo for Bayern football—or soccer, in American terms. Evan switches out his blue metallic eyeglasses for knockoff Ray-Bans—though poor Matthis complains that he can't see—and trades out his neon-green sneakers for old white tennis shoes that Matthis says have no "character."

"That's the point, mate," Evan says. "We need to fade into the woodwork."

For me, there's a blond wig with bangs that's not exactly flattering, a purple knit cap, burgundy lipstick that makes my fat lips look even bigger, and big Jackie O glasses. I also get a long, puffy gray coat (ugh) with a gray wool scarf, high-heeled black boots, and a grayish python-print hobo bag.

I come out of a stall after changing, and Evan is standing there texting on his smart phone. I take three steps in the boots and almost fall—have I mentioned that high heels are not my thing?

Evan looks up and shakes his head. "You really are

going to flunk deportment, aren't you?"

I glare at him. "Did you know that high heels were originally invented—by some French douche bag, I think—for, *men*?"

Evan shrugs, then smirks. "Well, it's a sign of intelligence, then, that we managed to pawn them off on women."

"No, I'll tell you what it's a sign of," I begin, but he locks himself in another stall to change into his own disguise. And he makes the mistake of thinking that the walls are more soundproof than they are, because he also makes a call. When Matthis, who's been washing his hands, turns off the water, we can overhear what he's saying.

"Cecily, I'm deadly serious."

I freeze. Evan is talking to my redheaded nemesis and his friend with benefits. And clearly she's part of our current problems.

"You'd better retract any statements you've given to management at GI," Evan says hotly. "This isn't about you or your ego—this is about getting a kid *killed* if you don't keep your bloody mouth shut."

I feel sick. He means Charlie, that much is obvious.

I realize what's happened. Abby has confided in Cecily, of all people. Hoping to impress her. And Cecily saw an opportunity to score at GI; prove that she's a badass just like her Interpol Agent parents. What damage is Cecily doing? And why?

"Back off, Cecily," Evan grinds out. There's a pause.

Then, "Are you really asking me that?"

Another pause.

Matthis and I look at each other.

"Cecily, your parents may be the Superman and Wonder Woman of Interpol when it comes to crimes against children, but you yourself have no experience, and you are not going to acquire it at the expense of Charlie Andrews's life. Understand?"

Evan's tone is scathing. He may be attracted to Roux (what guy wouldn't be?), but he clearly doesn't like her much.

"Now. You're going to go to the head office and tell them that you've made a mistake or gotten bad information. Yes, you bloody well are. Or I will reveal your colossal cock-up on the Renaud case to *everybody*. Really? Try me. This isn't a bluff; it's a promise. And stay the hell away from Abby. We all know you're just using her, and it's cruel."

There's not much more to the conversation. I quickly turn on the water at a different sink and pretend to wash my own hands, pretend that I haven't heard a word. I cast a sidelong glance at Matthis, and he nods once to indicate that he'll play dumb right along with me.

Evan emerges whistling from the bathroom stall a couple minutes later wearing a dark baseball cap, checked shirt over a navy tee, olive pants, and black snow boots. He looks like your average unremarkable Joe—the blue-blood Brit is gone.

"Miss me?" he asks.

I snort, but halfheartedly. My worry for Charlie is now off the charts. What if the kidnappers find out that Cecily has been talking? I tell myself that it's unlikely. That they can't have moles in GI.

"If it's any consolation, I think it's going to be just as hard for me to toddle around in these snow boots as it is for you to walk in those heels." Evan flashes me his innocent-as-the-Gerber-baby smile, as if he hasn't been threatening and blackmailing someone only moments ago.

"Huh." I so don't know how to feel about him. He's keeping secrets from me. But probably because he doesn't want me to worry. He handled Cecily flaw-lessly, but ruthlessly . . . and I don't want to think about how else he's handled her—up close and personally.

I'm silent as we roll up our old clothes and mash them into the shopping bag. Evan hands me the artist's portfolio to carry. It weighs a ton. "What's in here?" I ask. Whatever it is, it's metal and clanks.

"You'll find out soon enough."

He holds the door open for us, and we make our way out of the Augustiner Bräu as different people. The place is filling up as the afternoon goes on, and nobody notices us, not even our waitress, who's already picked up the euros we left on the table.

We walk north toward the Karlsplatz so that we can get lost among the people thronging the Christmas mar-ket set up there—row after row of colorful, packed-to-bursting stalls featuring handmade ornaments, sweets, trinkets, stuffed toy bears, hedgehogs, dolls, and other souvenirs. Evan tells us that in the summertime there's a large fountain in the center of the square, but I have a hard time picturing it.

The festive holiday atmosphere seems all wrong to me, with Charlie kidnapped and my parents halfway across the world, doing God only knows what. The stares of the carved wooden Kriss Kringles seem accusatory, the brown noses of the teddy bears ingratiating, the smiles of the too-blond dolls synthetic . . . they all tell me that Christmas is a fairy tale that I'll never enjoy again.

Yet I walk on with Matthis and Evan, praying for a miracle. Everyone else can have their tinsel, their trees, their stockings, and piles of gifts. All I want on December 25 is Charlie, safe with me back at the Paris Institute.

We walk quite a ways before we find what we're looking for: an unremarkably beige older-model Mercedes wagon that's conveniently unlocked and parked on a quiet side street. It's the perfect car to borrow, and its half tank of gas will get us to Murnau am Staffelsee with no problem.

It's an uneventful journey south through the white, snowy hills for about seventy kilometers to Murnau. The main street of the old town is a living, breathing postcard, an advertisement for the charm of German villages. There are cobblestones and quaint shops, timbered inns and cafés wafting woodsmoke from their chimneys, and microbreweries rich with polished wood and shiny copper tanks. There are bakeries bursting with pastries and confections. I see a little chocolate shop and think, with a pang, of Charlie.

Evan, full of odd information—who knows where he gets it?—tells us that it was once a spa town and the home of Der Blaue Reiter, a famous modern art movement. It seems to me that it's a strange place for a juvenile detention facility, but then Evan goes on to say that Murnau was also the site of a prison camp during the Second World War. Maybe they turned the facility into a juvie jail. Who knows?

We ditch the car outside a Tengelmann, a German grocery franchise, then walk a few blocks before checking into a tiny timber-framed *gasthaus* (German for bed-and-breakfast). It's a few blocks away from the juvie facility, which is a big, beige concrete structure surrounded by chain-link fence with loops of razor wire around the top.

"Cozy," Evan pronounces it.

I'd call it intimidating, myself. I have no idea how we're getting in there—I hope Rita's uncovered some helpful information on their security.

We sign into the *gasthaus* under assumed names, with another of Evan's credit cards and passports. He gets one room for Matthis and him and a separate one for me that's right next door.

I ask Evan if he's concerned that GI—or the bad guys, for that matter—may be tracing us through the credit cards and passports.

He gives me an angelic look. "They can't trace what they don't know about."

"But . . . then where did you get them?"

"Got my ways and means, love."

It's his standard answer. I shouldn't be surprised that Evan has somehow obtained multiple fake identities not issued by GI.

I throw open the door to my room. Ditching the heavy portfolio, I collapse on the big bed, exhausted, just as my cell phone rings. The ID says only "private caller." Wearily, I pull off my blond wig and punch the on button.

"Hello?"

"We warned you," says the menacing mechanical voice that called me in Paris. "Now Charlie will pay the price."

Chapter Eight

Ice. I turn to ice. My mouth works, but only a croak comes out. Then I manage the word "NO!" at full volume.

Evan and Matthis come running into my room and stare at me.

"What are you talking about?" I say rapidly into the phone. "I haven't involved police—"

"Don't lie to us. We have eyes everywhere."

"I'm not lying!"

"You sent your redheaded friend to the bosses at GI. That will cost your brother dearly."

"*No!*" I say again. My whole body starts to shake. "No, no. *Please*, don't hurt him."

Evan tries to grab the phone from me, but I dodge, feint, and hang on for dear life.

"I didn't send anyone to GI!" I insist. "I haven't told anyone—"

"Then who are the two boys you're with?"

"My roommate and a friend of Charlie's! I had to put together a team to help! Other than them, only Abby, my other roommate, knows . . . because she was there when you called and we couldn't just disappear on her."

"Charlie will lose the fingers on his left hand today, due to your carelessness. And perhaps an ear, if you don't contain this. Are we clear?"

"No! He's just a little boy! He's innocent. You can't hurt him—you can't be such a monster—"

Evan immobilizes my wrist, peels my fingers off the phone, and puts it on speaker. "This is Evan Kincaid, Kari's friend. How do you know about GI? It's top secret."

"We know everything, *Mister* Kincaid. We know that you're Rebecca Morrow's adopted son. We know that you're at Apprentice status in GI, with her as your mentor. We know that you're pushing to be an Initiate—to go on missions without her. Perhaps this is your chance to do that."

Evan's mouth tightens.

But I don't care about any of this. Tears stream down my face, and I could give a crap what these people know or how they know it. There's only one talking point in this conversation, as far as I'm concerned. "Don't hurt my brother. Please. I'll do whatever you ask . . . just don't hurt him."

I have this awful image of Charlie lying on his side on a dirty mattress in a dark basement. He's bound and gagged and filthy. His hair is matted and his nose is bloody.

"You *will* do whatever we ask, Karina." The mechanical

voice is menacing. "So will your friends. And now, here's a little motivation for you—"

An earsplitting shriek comes over the speaker. It's prolonged, heart-wrenching, bloodcurdling—I can't even describe it. It's the worst thing I've ever heard, and I cannot control my reaction.

Suddenly I'm screaming and crying and cussing and begging all at the same time. And I'm fighting Evan for the phone. "Wild" is not the word for me. It doesn't cover it.

"Christ," Evan exclaims, before tossing the phone to a freaked-out Matthis.

I'm still screaming as Evan tackles me onto the bed. "I will kill you! Don't you touch my brother again! Don't touch him! I will kill you!"

Evan rolls me over and sits on me before I can hurt him. He yells toward the phone.

"Listen! Listen to her. You want her this way? She is of *no use* to you if you do this. Understand?"

"Get her under control," the mechanical voice says.

"I can't do that, unless you stop what you're doing. Lay another hand on that child and I'll have to check Kari into a mental hospital."

Silence.

I'm crying hysterically. "Charlie!" I keep screaming, over and over.

"Do you hear me?" Evan shouts in the direction of the phone.

More silence.

Evan says, his voice hard and cold, "I have already shut down the leak that's occurred on our end. I will make sure the information is contained and come up with a cover story so that you don't have GI and all of Interpol breathing down your necks. But in return, please—*please* promise that you won't hurt Charlie."

A long pause ensues.

"You have twelve hours," the voice says at last. "Twelve hours. After that, Charlie loses not just his fingers, but his hands and feet."

This pronouncement is followed by a dial tone.

"Christ," Evan says again.

Matthis drops the phone as if it's poisoned.

And I keep sobbing incoherently and struggling to get up.

"Matthis, bring me that small black bag," Evan orders.

I'm guessing Matthis complies, because the next words out of Evan's mouth are, "Thanks. Unzip it. Give me— yeah. Uncap it."

I feel a sharp pinch, then a burning sensation as a needle goes into my arm. "Nooooo! Damn it, Evan, you have no right to do that—"

But my lips stop working, and things go really fuzzy.

There's regret in his eyes and in the twist of his mouth as he rolls me onto my back and looks down at me, as he cups my cheek with one hand and cradles his own phone with another. A touch of his thumb and he's speed-dialing someone.

"Yeah, Kincaid here," he says tersely. His eyes are flinty and his jaw's like granite. "We have a situation. . . ."

And those are the last words I hear before darkness closes in.

◇ ◇ ◇

When I return to consciousness, I'm disoriented for a moment. I can't remember where exactly I am. I stare at a pale blue silk lampshade, then at a painting of a seascape, then into a gilt-framed mirror—one that happens to reflect the image of Matthis on his laptop, fingers flying over the keyboard.

That's when it all comes roaring back to me. Charlie is in the hands of kidnappers, and they're torturing him. They're saying they'll cut off his fingers, hands, and feet. They've threatened to send me his head in a box. . . .

How can I be this terrified and yet this weary simultaneously?

Add furious to the mix as I remember Evan jabbed a needle into my arm and sedated me—with Charlie's life in danger.

"Where is he?" I yell at Matthis. "Where is the rat?"

Poor Matthis jerks, startled, and drops his laptop on the floor.

Evan pokes his head out of the bathroom. There's water running, and he's got toothpaste around his mouth. "I presume you mean me?"

"You're damn straight I mean you!" I jump off the bed. "How could you? How could you drug me at a time like this?"

"I did what had to be done," Evan says. He disappears back into the bathroom. I hear the toothbrush scrubbing away at his teeth.

Unbelievable.

I march straight into the bathroom, snatch up a paper

cup that's on the sink, and throw the contents—water—into his face.

It runs down his forehead, nose, and cheeks. He says absolutely nothing.

Neither do I.

It's Matthis who gives a shrill whistle, then shakes his head.

We ignore him.

Eventually he goes back to his laptop, his fingers clattering over the keys.

Evan stares at me evenly, then with deliberate slowness he reaches for a hand towel and mops at his face. "That was refreshing," he says. "Feel better?"

That's when I try my best to kick him in the balls. But I'm still muzzy and half-drugged, and Evan's got very quick reflexes. He grabs my foot and holds on. "Don't do that again."

"I will!" I yell at him. "How can you knock me out and then stand there brushing your freakin' teeth while Charlie's being tortured?!" I try to jerk my foot out of his grasp, to no avail.

"Did you shave, too? Put on cologne? Because of course you've got to look all GQ while these people are killing my brother!"

"They're not killing him. And you need to get ahold of yourself, Kari." He says this forcefully. "You are no good to Charlie in this overly emotional state. As for whether I shaved or not—yes, I did. To kill some time until you woke up. Is that a crime?"

"I wouldn't have been unconscious if not for you!" I

finally wrest my foot out of his grasp and stomp it to the ground. "And yes, I believe it *is* a crime to drug people without their permission."

"Great. You can have me prosecuted later. For now, you need to trust me."

I gape at him, then laugh in his face. "Trust you? Trust the person who just sat on me and jabbed a needle into my arm?"

"Yes." He stands there looking reasonable and relaxed, his arms hanging loosely by his sides. Acting as if I'm the irrational one, not him—the guy who's been carrying around a syringe full of God knows what.

"Why should I trust you? Why the hell are you packing needles and sedatives, anyway? Who were you planning to use them on?"

He shrugs. "Anyone I needed to incapacitate. I also carry zip ties—but you didn't object to those when they came in handy."

"What else do you have, Evan? A shovel? A tarp? Lime?"

"Very funny. Kari, you know me. You know my background. You know what I'm training to be—"

"Do I?"

"Yes." His gaze is calm and steady and blue . . . and oddly enough, I find my anger dissipating. He seems to sense that.

"Kari. You need to trust me."

And unwillingly, I do. I think about everything Evan has done for me and for Charlie over the past few months. We wouldn't be in the GI program if not for him. We'd be in foster care. Separated.

He raises his eyebrows. "All right?"

Reluctantly, I nod. There are times when Evan makes me crazy. There are times when I hate him. There are times when I cannot stand the fact that my stupid body seems to be attracted to him. But facts are facts: He may piss me off, but he's never let me down.

Not once.

He nods back. "Good. Now, just to give you a quick update, everything's been taken care of at GI. The alarm that Cecily raised—it's fine now."

"Fine? Taken care of? How? And would you even have told me about it if the kidnappers hadn't?"

He sighs.

"Yeah, I didn't think so." I glare at him.

"I'll explain everything later. The *Reader's Digest* version is that I made some calls."

"Made some calls? But—"

"Later, Kari. Right now, it's good that you woke up on your own, because we've got to get going. Rita Skyped in while you were asleep, with some good information. The juvie facility is actually relinquishing Gustav Duvernay to French officials in just a few hours. Very early tomorrow morning, he'll be transported by van to a small private airfield right outside of Munich, where they'll be flying him to Paris for trial. We need to snatch him before he makes it to the plane."

I open and then close my mouth. "Tomorrow morning?"

"Yes. And we've got a lot of setup and surveillance to do before then. So we need to leave. Now."

"But Evan, the kidnappers only gave us twelve hours!" I'm starting to panic again.

"You've been out less than two. It's after nine p.m. now. They'll be transporting Gustav at five a.m."

I do the math. "Evan, that takes us to less than two hours to grab Gustav before they h-h-hurt Charlie. What if something goes wrong? What if we fail?"

Evan looks at me grimly. He walks over and puts his hands on my shoulders. The irises of his eyes have gone an intense, dark blue. "We are absolutely not going to fail. I refuse to let that happen. So let's go pick up the very large lorry that Matthis has obligingly located for us."

"Lorry?" I'm bewildered.

"Truck. I'll explain on the way."

Chapter Nine

We leave the *gasthaus* in our disguises and carry backpacks that contain clothing and ski masks. Once we're
back on the street, Matthis and I go hang out in a café
while Evan makes his way to a local Swiss dairy franchise that has a small fleet of delivery trucks. There,
he "borrows" one and returns to meet us in the alley
behind the coffee shop.

The truck is painted to look like a giant black-and-
white cow, with the headlights as eyes—complete with
eyelashes—and even a tail delineated on the back door.
If I weren't so worried about Charlie, I might laugh.

Matthis and I quickly crawl into the back, which
smells strongly of cheese. So strongly that I'm afraid
I'll be sick. And I will probably have nightmares about
drowning in a bowl of fondue or suffocating in a giant
grilled-cheese sandwich.

As we ditch our disguises and change into plain black clothing, I say to Evan, *"This* is your idea of an urban assault vehicle?"

"What, I should have stolen a city bus? Maybe a limo for your ladyship? This is completely innocuous and unmemorable. Who will question a dairy truck making early morning rounds?"

"I just want to know if we're delivering milk on the way to grab Gustav."

"Very funny. I like this truck. I'm calling her Spot," Evan says.

Spot? Seriously?

The truck is very clean inside, despite the smell. Matthis and I hang on for dear life to a couple of straps bolted to the wall as Evan takes a corner too quickly and accelerates.

"Matthis, how's it coming with the traffic lights near the airfield?"

"I'm in, thanks to Rita. It's a little tricky with the timing, but I can pull it off. We'll stop the police van here—" He turns the screen of his laptop to face me and points. "Then detour it to this back road, which will dead-end into roadblock barriers that we'll put partially into position now—as soon as we grab them."

"What about other traffic on the road?" I'm anxious.

Matthis shakes his head. "It's very unlikely between the hours of ten p.m. and five a.m. The only people who'd take such a rural route are residents of little farmhouses out there, and I'm betting they'll be in bed."

"But what if they're not?" I persist. I'm so afraid something will go wrong and Charlie will be hurt.

"Kari, don't worry. The barriers will be off to the side until we push them into place around four thirty a.m. So nobody will pay much attention to them. Plus Rita's hacked into the telephone company's system, and she'll see to it that the phone lines are down. She'll also jam the cell coverage here, just to be safe. That way nobody can call out—not even the guards on the transport truck."

"Okay," I say. "But how—and where—are we getting roadblock barriers, exactly?"

Evan chuckles. "That's our next stop." He pulls over the dairy truck and puts the transmission in neutral. "Your turn to drive, sweetheart. I've got to change clothes."

I balk. "I've never driven a truck of this size—"

"Time to learn," Evan says cheerfully. "Anyway, it's easy as long as you don't have to reverse or parallel park. Neither of which you'll be doing."

"Great . . ."

Evan gets out of the driver's seat, already peeling off his shirt, and we awkwardly slide by each other in order to change places. I completely ignore his six-pack abs, thank you very much. I most certainly do not examine his insanely buff upper arms, which are about the circumference of my thighs.

Evan clearly works out more than your average guy—much more than Luke, though I remind myself that Luke's legs are better because of the sprints and hurdles he does in track. Evan lifts weights, probably with hordes of drooling girls slyly checking him out . . . kind of like right now. *Stop it, Kari!*

Let's just say that it's no surprise that, with arms like his, Evan was able to choke me unconscious in record time.

I slip into the driver's seat of the dairy truck, buckle the seat belt, and grip the wheel. I do not think about Evan taking his pants off in the back. I step firmly on the gas. There's a roar as the engine revs, but we don't move an inch.

"It helps to take it out of neutral, darling." Evan's voice betrays his rich amusement at my expense. "And, though I love the appreciative audience, keep your eyes on the road."

I do hate him, after all.

I slam the gearshift into drive and hit the gas hard again, so that the half-naked jerk is thrown against the wall of the truck.

"Would someone like to tell me where the hell we're going?" I ask sweetly, trying to get used to the heaviness and clunkiness of maneuvering this giant rectangular cow on wheels. It's not like driving any car I've ever had the privilege to borrow.

"There's a construction site ahead," Evan says. "Take the next right and the third right after that. Then drive for about two miles. The place will be on the left. They're building some kind of municipal hall, and they've got some handy barricades up that we'll just pop into the back of Spot here."

"Fine," I say. "What about the detour signs, though?"

"Snagged two of them yesterday in Munich. They're in the artist's portfolio."

"When?"

"When I was rounding up our disguises." Evan, now fully dressed, comes up front and sits next to me, in the passenger seat.

"I'm feeling a little inadequate in the face of your ingenuity," I say.

"Don't. You're doing an excellent job of terrifying us with your driving so that we can't be nervous about ambushing three armed guards, so thanks for that."

Matthis chortles at that one.

Aaarrghh! Have I mentioned lately that I *do* hate Evan Kincaid?

Furious, I take the next right, as instructed.

"What, you're going to let me live after that statement?" Evan inquires politely.

"No. I'm just trying to decide the best way to kill you," I assure him.

"You'd best wait until after we get Gustav. You need my help with the guards."

In the end, it's both easier and harder than I thought it would be. It's simple to grab the road barriers and toss them into Spot the Dairy Truck. Before dropping them off, we do surveillance on the detour road for an hour, and Matthis is right—it remains deserted and trouble-free.

The hardest part of the whole operation, for me, is

the waiting. The night is also freezing cold—only to be expected in December in Germany--and it begins to snow with a vengeance. It looks like a picture post-card outside, with twinkling lights everywhere and the trees loaded down with tufts of snow. But this fairy-tale comes with a windchill factor of about minus twenty.

Poor skinny Matthis's bones are practically clacking together as he shivers uncontrollably. My teeth chatter, and we can all see our breath as we exhale. I wish we'd taken the comforters off the beds in the *gasthaus* and brought them with us.

Though initially I thought the ski masks were a little melodramatic, I'm thankful for them now—except that my nose is still getting frostbite. I'm sure of it. I rub at it, and then at my arms.

Matthis is crouched in his praying mantis stance, his eyes glued to the screen of his laptop. He's tracking the transport truck via a GPS chip. When I ask Evan how we got a GPS tracker on the truck in the first place, he smiles mysteriously and says that he's got friends in low places.

"Okay, people," Matthis says tersely. "Our boy is half a mile away."

We moved the barriers into position and put up the detour signs roughly thirty minutes ago; it's now 5:17 a.m.

One hour and forty-seven minutes until those bas-tards hurt Charlie—or not. Depending on me. On us. Every fiber of my being is knotted; every nerve ending is vibrating with anxiety.

Evan touches my shoulder. "It's going to be just fine. All right?"

I close my eyes and nod.

Evan straps on a motorcycle helmet, just in case the collision is really bad. He doesn't want to kill the driver or the other guards, just stun them or knock them out. Of course, there are no guarantees—crashing one vehicle into another isn't an exact science.

Not to mention that it's very dangerous.

"Be safe," I say.

"I'll try." He gives me a wry twist of his lips—the ghost of a smile. I just hope the rest of him isn't a ghost before this little maneuver is complete. . . .

"Here they come!" Matthis announces. "Okay, changing the light at the corner: It's now red. Kari, time for us to get into position."

Matthis shoves the laptop into his backpack and shrugs it on. I flex my fingers in their thin leather gloves and make sure I have the zip ties in my back pocket. Then we jump from the back of the van and hide in the trees at the ambush point. Evan starts the engine, revs it, and waits, making sure Spot's "eyes," the headlights of the dairy truck, are off. We've covered the taillights and the running lights with black electric tape so that nothing gives us away.

"And . . . game time!" Matthis whispers.

Sure enough, a silver-colored van with a wide, dark blue stripe and POLIZEI emblazoned on the side turns the corner, slowly, somewhat cautiously. Clearly the driver wasn't expecting the detour. He may even be trying to call in to management to let them know what's happening. Of course, he won't be able to get through, courtesy of Rita.

Before we can even catch our breath, Evan roars out of the darkness and slams Spot's passenger side into the driver's side of the transport van, roughly at the front left wheel.

The noise is explosive; deafening. My heart literally feels as if it's jumped out of my ribs and is trying to hurl itself past my esophagus. I almost choke on it as I run out of the trees toward the rear sliding door of the police van. As I wrench it open, I practically sob with relief as Evan jumps out of the driver's side of Spot, unharmed. The passenger's side door is history, crumpled beyond recognition.

"Go!" he shouts.

I pull a stunned guard out of the transport van, head-butt him to add to his shock, and then give him a good chop in the windpipe. He falls to the ground, clutching his neck. Before he can react further, I grab his gun and train it on him.

"Hands behind your back!" I yell, straddling him at the hips.

I jerk his left arm behind him, jam the muzzle of the gun behind his right ear, and repeat my order. He obeys. I zip-tie his wrists. Then I bind his ankles together with more of the electric tape. It's handy stuff.

Evidently the driver's been knocked unconscious. His head smacked the windshield and then the steering wheel. He's covered in blood but still breathing, with a fairly regular pulse.

Evan, Matthis, and I move cautiously toward the back of the transport van, where a third guard sits inside with the prisoner.

Evan gestures for the two of us to get low to the ground. Then he tosses a rock at the handles of the doors.

Shots ring out immediately. The guard inside is panicked, and who can blame him?

This isn't good news. The shots are loud, overpoweringly so, and sound exactly like what they are. Neighbors are probably being woken up. Neighbors who may or may not come running.

"Put down your weapon!" Evan bellows. "Put it down on the floor—and we won't hurt you."

Two more shots ring out.

"Shit," Matthis says. He's trembling from head to toe, whether from adrenaline or cold, it's hard to say. Maybe from both.

"Stay low," snaps Evan.

One last time, he yells at the guard inside. "We won't hurt you. We just want Gustav."

The door of the van flies open, and a last bullet goes whizzing past Evan's head as he curses a blue streak.

Then a dark, rumpled figure erupts from the back of the vehicle and starts running. Awkwardly, with his hands in front of him.

"What the—?" I see a flash of silver in the moonlight—handcuffs—before the figure trips and falls on his face in the snow. The gun he was holding goes flying. "It's

Gustav!" I shout. "He's escaping!" I hurtle after him, wondering what's happened to the guard.

Within six strides, I've caught up to Duvernay. I leap onto his shoulders, knocking him facedown once again as he tries to get up. Because of my forward momentum, I somehow end up astride his neck, his head between my thighs. "Freeze!" I yell.

I know that not even cops say that in real life—only in the movies—but somehow it comes out of my mouth.

Gustav raises his face from the snow. *"Une fille?"* he says. He starts to laugh.

Then he rolls suddenly to the side, knocking me off-balance and back onto his chest. "A *pretty* girl." He grins. It's the dirtiest, most disreputable grin imaginable, not least because it's surrounded by a lot of beard stubble. Duvernay hasn't seen a razor in a while, and he has wicked, dancing green eyes rimmed by long, sooty lashes.

"My luck has changed! What better place to be, zan out of jail and between a pretty girl's legs?"

I'm completely mortified. But oddly paralyzed. I'm not even sure how much time has gone by when a male throat clears somewhere above my left shoulder. "You want to get off our new friend, Kari?" Evan's voice is dry.

"Vraiment, zere is no need for her to move, if she is comfortable." Gustav's eyes twinkle, and his grin gets even filthier—if that's possible.

My entire body flash-fries—from the tips of my ears down to my toes. I jump up so fast that I kick snow into his face. I am positively pulsing with embarrassment. And our buddy the thief is enjoying it.

Strangely enough, Evan isn't the slightest bit amused. "Gustav Duvernay, I presume? Thief at large?"

"How do you know I am a thief?" Gustav demands.

"How did you choke out the guard?" Evan asks at the same time.

Gustav lifts an eyebrow and holds up his handcuffs, which flash silver again in the moonlight. "Zey are both a hindrance and a help."

"We know you're a thief because we've been assigned to break you out," I inform him. "By some very bad people who are holding my little brother hostage and threatening to dismember him."

Our new friend's full lips compress and flatten into a straight, uncompromising line.

"They said that you'd know what to do next," I add. "They want us to steal something, with your help."

"*Merde*," he says under his breath.

Okay, so in addition to *"douche"* and *"moi,"* I know the word *"merde."* It means "shit." See. My French improves every day.

"What time is it, Evan? How can we let the kidnappers know that we have Gustav?"

"I'm sure they'll call us."

I stare at him, suddenly petrified. "They can't! Oh my God! Evan, Rita's knocked out the cell coverage. We have to go—we have to get to an area where they can reach me!"

As if on cue, police sirens split the predawn air.

Evan hauls Gustav to his feet. Then he recovers the gun from a few feet away.

"Matthis!" I scream. And we all start running.

Running for Charlie's life, for our liberty, and in pursuit of whatever it is that Gustav will help us steal.

Chapter Ten

The sirens are getting louder, meaning the cops will be here any second. Spot the Dairy Truck is incapacitated. We've got to borrow a car—*now*.

My breath comes in ragged gasps as we tear through the snow. We must get to a place with cell phone coverage. Immediately. *Yesterday*. My body shakes as I think about the consequences to Charlie if the kidnappers call and I don't answer.

Turns out Matthis is quite the sprinter. I think he could give Luke a good run for his money. Evan and I can barely keep up with him, even in our full-on panic, as we hurdle a sagging, weathered fence and go flying up the gravel drive of one of the farmhouses.

We scare a couple of hens and a goat in a small pen near what's probably a vegetable garden under the snow. Unfortunately, as we might have guessed, most farmhouses come complete with a farmer inside, and this one is no exception.

We spot an old Saab sitting near the house, and Evan wrenches the driver's side door open while Matthis and Gustav scramble into the backseat. I go for the shotgun position next to Evan.

"Bon, on se casse!" says Gustav.

I stare at him. "Huh?"

"Let's get out of here!" he translates.

An old man with crazy white hair comes running out of the kitchen in his bathrobe. *"Halt!"* He yells.

Evan pulls the guard's gun on him and takes aim as he responds. "Go back inside! We won't hurt you. We just need to take the car. Okay?"

The man stops in his tracks and puts his hands in the air. He babbles something incoherent.

"Back into the house!" Evan repeats. "Kari, get this thing hot-wired. NOW."

I look down. "The keys are in the ignition, genius."

Gustav snorts. *"Andouille."*

Huh? What does sausage have to do with anything?

"Right," Evan says, handing me the gun and starting the engine. He glances at Gustav in the rearview mirror. *"Branleur."*

Gustav laughs.

Evan sees my puzzled expression and explains, "He called me a dork. I called him good-for-nothing."

"Like we have time for insults?" I throw up my hands.

Then the car's in gear and we're hurtling backward, spraying gravel at the unlucky, bewildered farmer, who gets only three steps toward his kitchen door before his plump, enraged wife runs out, yelling.

Evan wrenches the wheel to the left, fishtailing the Saab, and then hits the gas. We zoom down the dirt road that leads away from the farmhouse, just as two German police cars fly by.

Though I personally think it would have been better to drive normally and not attract attention to ourselves, Evan careens onto the main road and takes the speedometer from forty to eighty kilometers per hour in a few seconds—pretty impressive for this old Saab. It's got to be at least twenty years old and stinks of mildew and motor oil.

The sun is coming up, and it's blinding as it hits the layer of grime and ice on the windshield that we're trying to scrape off with the wipers. Evan has to stick his head out the window to see as we head back to A95 and Munich.

"Why are you driving toward the highway?" I yell. "We have a better chance of outrunning or losing them on rural roads."

"Really?" Evan shouts back. "On *icy, mountainous* rural roads? And what happens if we collide with something or smash through a guardrail and fall to our deaths? No thanks. We'll take our chances in the city, and we've a better chance of escape there once we abandon the car."

Mr. Know-it-all puts the pedal to the metal, and I fumble for a seat belt. Okay, so he's got a valid argument. And there will be better cell coverage in Munich. I check my phone every five seconds, praying that the little bars will return—the bars that mean I have a connection. Nothing so far.

We get to A95 without incident, and about ten minutes down the road, I almost cry with relief as the bars return and there's no message indicating a missed call.

I calm down a bit as we go a good forty-five minutes without seeing a single *polizei* car.

But my worries about how we shouldn't have called attention to ourselves are valid, because one of the German police cars we saw must have radioed to buddies outside Munich. A cruiser gains on us rapidly, sirens wailing.

"Evan, he's right on our tail!"

"Yes, I can see that." We're nearing the outskirts of the city. Evan wrenches the wheel left, taking us onto the Fraunhoferstrasse, and then right onto Mullerstrasse. Gamely, the German cop follows. Evan zooms left down Corneliusstrasse and then careens right onto Blumenstrasse. We've now entered the circuit that runs around historic old Munich, since this street turns into the Ringstrasse.

In the backseat, Matthis has landed on Gustav, who unceremoniously shoves him off. "I prefer girls," he says, winking at me and producing that dirty smile again.

Matthis squints at him and mumbles, "Don't flatter yourself, man."

The Ring is crowded with cars and buses, despite the early hour. We get stuck in traffic, and the German cop wrenches open his door, clearly intending to jump out and confront us.

"*Merde!*" yells Gustav as Evan spins the wheel to

the right, rocketing the Saab up onto the sidewalk and through a sea of bistro tables and chairs outside a café. Luckily, only a couple of people are sitting out there—it's too cold.

A woman shrieks, grabs her dog, and jumps out of the way.

We lurch forward, two wheels on the sidewalk as business owners blanch, scramble into their doorways, shout, and point at us.

A quick glance back reveals that the cop is stunned and slack-jawed but pulling onto the sidewalk after us.

"Go, Evan!" I shout.

Matthis makes a noise of sheer terror before ducking his head and assuming a crash-landing position in the backseat.

Gustav, however, seems to be enjoying himself. His eyes hold a certain sparkle, and an odd smile plays around his lips. I realize that he's an adrenaline junkie.

I'm distracted from my observations about our new buddy, though, when Evan takes us screaming, on two wheels, into a hairpin left turn into a crowded food market. We literally run over a pedestrian's foot. I wince as the guy screams in agony.

"Bollocks," Evan mutters before diving suddenly right, down a side street. That'd be a great move, except that it's a one-way side street, and we are flying down it in the wrong direction. Toward a city bus, no less.

Matthis chooses this moment to pop his head up. He screams, a high unnatural sound that comes close to rupturing my eardrums.

The bus is huge, it's bright green, and it's about to flatten the Saab.

I open my own mouth to shriek—can't help it—when Evan wrenches the wheel right and we go barreling into a small parking garage next to an office building. The bus, its driver leaning savagely on the horn, misses us by maybe three inches.

Gustav cackles maniacally from the backseat. *"C'est ouf!"*

"That's crazy!" My brain supplies the translation automatically. I guess I've picked up more French than I thought. Who knew?

A corner of Evan's mouth lifts. "Thank you," he says—before our next big problem comes into view. A car is slowly backing out of a slot, right into our path.

Evan can't slow down—there's no time.

We hit the oblivious driver, smashing him right back into his parking place and shattering a taillight.

"Oops," Evan says.

We fly up the ramp without stopping, circling round and round the garage.

I'm cautiously optimistic that we've lost the German cop, but I'm wrong. As we take the next turn, I'm able to look down a couple of levels. I spot the officer's car, still in dogged pursuit.

"He's still behind us! Guys, the only way we're going to lose him is to switch out the car," I say. "Evan, pull into the next spot you see. Then everyone rolls out. Stay down. Crawl under at least the next three cars, okay? Then I'll find one that we can steal."

Evan thinks about it, then nods decisively. He jerks his head toward Gustav. "Watch him, though. He's still hampered by the handcuffs, but he may try to run again."

"*Mais non!*" Gustav protests. "I'm 'aving too much fun weeth you." He says this with a delighted smile.

Evan squeals the poor abused Saab into the next slot he sees, and we open the doors, slide out, and belly crawl. Gustav has a harder time than the rest of us, given that he's doing it in cuffs, but he's surprisingly agile.

We shimmy under a Peugeot, a Volkswagen, and a weird little car I can't identify. The one after that is a BMW 7 Series.

"Let's have that one, shall we?" Evan inclines his head toward it.

"Fine." I pop up, slim jim already in hand. It takes me about three seconds to get the door open and pop the other door locks.

"*T'es trop fort!*" Gustav says, admiration in his eyes. "*Je me la ferais bien.*"

I don't know what this means, but clearly the guys do. Matthis blushes.

Evan's mouth tightens, but he says nothing.

Gustav's green eyes dance as we scramble into the Beemer.

Evan's back in the driver's seat, but thoughtfully he turns to me. "Kari, you drive. I'll duck down in the front seat. You too, guys," he tosses into the back. "That way she'll appear to be a woman alone. The cop will be looking for four of us."

This change of plan necessitates Evan and I switching

places. We don't have time to get out of the car—the cop might spot us, and he's close behind. So Evan grabs me, hauls me into his lap, and then slides out from under me and into the passenger seat, depositing me into the driver's. I'm both annoyed and secretly . . . thrilled? Turned on? What's the word? . . . at the ease with which he picks me up.

Stop it, Kari.

Then he somehow folds himself into position on the floor so that he's hidden from a casual observer.

I get down to business and hot-wire the car, but my anxiety surges again.

When will the kidnappers call? *When?* We're twenty minutes past the twelve-hour window they gave us. My throat tightens.

Focus, Kari. Focus.

"Twist your hair up into a knot," Evan orders. "You want to look like a businesswoman, not a schoolgirl."

I do that, then slowly back the BMW out of its spot, conveniently right into the path of the German cop. What timing!

He leans on his horn.

I fake being startled and throw up my hands. Then I pull back into the spot and he screams by me in his blue-and-silver-painted cruiser.

"Bye-bye, *polizei*," I murmur. Then I reverse again and drive us all out of the parking garage. We're clear.

"That cop's not too bright if he cruised right by the parked Saab," Matthis observes.

"He'll figure it out within a matter of minutes," Evan

says tersely. "Kari, get us back out to the Ringstrasse, and cross Maximilianstrasse, the luxury shopping street. Go right onto . . ."—he consults the GPS on his smart phone—"Burkleinstrasse, then left on Saint Anna. Get us good and lost over there before he remembers that the BMW is the car that left the garage. Okay?"

"Yep." I concentrate on driving. The streets are narrow and bustling with activity. All around us, modern life is oddly juxtaposed with history—part of Europe's charm.

"Okay, we're turning onto the Burkleinstrasse."

"Good. Let's get closer to the Haus der Kunst, the art museum. We'll get rid of the car near there, hop on the subway, connect with the train station, and get out of Munich."

"Sounds like a plan." My pulse is back to normal, but I glance compulsively at my watch every minute or so. *When* are the kidnappers going to call again? And when they do, will they let me talk to Charlie?

My mouth dries as I think about what they could be doing to him. My heart begins to pound again. My palms are suddenly sweaty on the steering wheel.

I've pulled up to the next traffic light when my cell phone vibrates in my back pocket. I snatch it and press the on button. "Hello?"

The mechanically altered voice asks, "Do you have Duvernay?"

"Yes," I say breathlessly. "We have him. Let me speak to Charlie. Please."

"I need proof that you have the thief. Take a picture of him and text it to me." The voice gives a number to me.

"Wait—I don't have anything to write it down—"

"Then you'd better remember it, Karina." And the line goes dead.

Frantically, I hit the camera icon on my phone and turn around to take a picture of Gustav. That's when I see the German cop, gun drawn, approaching us from the rear.

Chapter Eleven

Gustav doesn't want his picture taken and starts to argue. Then he freezes as he registers my panicked expression.

Evan, too, sees my distress. "Kari, what is it?"

"The German cop. He's right behind us. Coming up to the BMW."

"On foot?"

"Yes."

"Pull over to the side of the street. Then get out of the car—with your hands visible—and start talking. Distract him. I'll come around behind him and take him down."

"But Evan—there are people everywhere! How—"

"Out of the car, Kari. Just do it. I'll take care of the rest."

I'm shaking from head to toe. Not just because of the cop—but because I need to send that picture of Gustav to the kidnappers already. And this is going to cause a delay. What if the delay costs Charlie a hand or a foot?

But I get out of the car.

"*Halt, Fraulein!*" the cop shouts. "*Polizei! Hände hoch!*"

"Oh, God, officer—did I do something wrong?" I babble at him. "Did I not signal back at the intersection? Is a taillight out? What's the problem?" I hold my hands in the air and look as dumb as I can possibly manage to.

He's short, with gingery hair, freckles, and blue eyes. He looks more like a choirboy than a cop. He also looks extremely pissed off. He demands my driver's license.

"No problem," I say—even though I have no intention of giving it to him. "Let me get my purse?"

The words are no sooner out of my mouth than Evan materializes next to the guy, holding a jacket over the gun we took off the transport truck guard. "Apologies for this, mate," he says with a wry, sincere smile. "But this is a Heckler and Koch nine-millimeter, it's fully loaded, and I'm prepared to use it if you don't let the lady get back into the BMW."

The young cop's eyes bulge.

"Let's not make a public scene," Evan continues. "We're both going to walk over and get into your vehicle and go for a drive. I won't harm you as long as you do as you're told. I'll eventually leave you parked behind the Haus der Kunst, where you will take a little nap. When you awaken, it's entirely up to you whether you tell your superior officer how a bunch of kids got the drop on you. All right?"

Evan turns to me. "Back into the car. Take and send the photo."

I don't need to be told twice. I jump back into the BMW and turn to face Gustav.

I aim my phone at him, and he starts to protest again—after all, a thief doesn't want too many pictures of himself out there—but then he registers the expression on my face. It tells him that if I have to kill him, then toe-tag his body before I photograph him, I will. So Gustav obligingly mugs for the camera as the cop moves with Evan back to his car. The officer is clearly not a happy camper, but he doesn't resist.

My hands are shaking so badly that I have to take two pictures of Gustav because I know the first one is a blur. The number that the kidnappers gave me is burned into my brain, but I can barely get the digits punched into the keypad. At last I manage to hit send, right as the phone rings in my hand.

"Hello!" I almost screech the word.

"Do you know what a band saw is, Karina?" I hear a horrible industrial motor sound.

"I just sent the photo! I sent it! Don't hurt Charlie—"

"Kaaa-riiiii!" It's a scream of sheer terror, it's definitely Charlie's voice, and his fear clearly trumps mine. I collapse over the seat back. My words run together, into a soup of anguish. "No-no-no-don't-hurt-him-please-please-just-let-him-go-he's-seven-years-old—"

The awful industrial motor noise starts again; then comes another shriek from my brother.

Matthis opens the back door of the Beemer and pukes onto the pavement.

"Mon Dieu!" Gustav leans forward, grabs the phone from my hand, and punches the speaker button, shouting volubly in French. It's so rapid that I can't make out the words. But I do hear him say his name, then something else that sounds scathing, along with, *un petit garcon*, which I know to mean "small boy."

There's a blessed silence on the line—no more screams, no more industrial motor. And then the mechanical voice says, "I'd adjust your attitude, if I were you, Monsieur Duvernay. Or you won't like the consequences to another guest of ours."

A shadow of fear crosses Gustav's face.

"Karina," the voice says, "Charlie will remain safe as long as you execute the next task. You have seventy-two hours to do so." The line goes dead.

Gustav hands me back the phone. He shakes his head, makes a concerned, clucking noise that is peculiarly European, and then reaches out to wipe the tears from under my eyes with his thumb. "We will do zis theeng, okay? For your brother. And for—" He breaks off, looking grim.

"For what? What did he mean by another guest?"

Gustav dismisses my question with a Gallic wave of his hand. "Do not weep, eh?"

I nod and try to pull myself together. If not for me, then for Charlie.

I put the car into gear and pull it away from the curb, merging into traffic. I drive around the block and circle back to a street that I'm pretty sure will take us to the Haus der Kunst, where Evan will be waiting for us with the snoozing cop. Maybe I'm not so judgmental about him carrying needles and sedatives any longer—it goes without saying that the cop won't go to sleep on his own.

Abducting and drugging a cop at gunpoint is probably a very big no-no in Germany, or anywhere else. I don't want to think about the charges Evan may be facing on my behalf. Somehow he's truly become my white knight.

"You are too pretty to cry," Gustav says, interrupting my train of thought.

I don't know how to respond to this, so I make a sound that's half donkey bray and half snort. I glance into the rearview mirror and see Matthis roll his eyes.

"What *is* this thing we have to do?" I ask around a sniffle.

Gustav gives me a Gallic shrug. "I am a thief, eh? So. They want me to steal something."

"But what?"

He smiles. "They call it *jungbrunnen*. Ze fountain of youth."

"Excuse me?"

"*Oui*, of course." He doesn't understand that I'm asking for clarification.

"No, I mean—I *mean*, what do *you* mean by 'fountain of youth'?"

"It is an ingredient—highly sought after, you understand—recently discovered by a famous French cosmetics company: Jolie, Inc. You are familiar with zis company?"

"Of course." How can I not be? Even though makeup is not exactly my thing, the Jolie brand is in every department store in America.

"Ze ingredient—it is for rejuvenating ze skin, yes? But better and faster than anything on ze market. A miracle, zey call it."

"But why steal it? Why not just figure out the formula and duplicate it?" Matthis asks.

"This is exactly their goal. But zey need ze ingredient first, *tu comprends*? In order to analyze ze chemical compounds. *Voilà*, they say. 'Gustav, steal it, *s'il vous plait*—'"

"So let me get this straight," I interrupt. "All this fuss is about a freaking *wrinkle cream*? That's . . . idiotic."

Gustav gives me his shrug.

"And it doesn't make sense."

He shrugs again.

"So we have to break into the Zurich headquarters of Jolie, Inc.?"

Gustav smiles engagingly. *"Mais oui."*

I almost run over a curb as I pull into the parking area of the art museum. "There's no way." Jolie, Inc. will be more difficult to get into than the Agency. At least the Agency was used to the occasional tour group.

I park the car, then turn around to face Gustav.

He tilts his head and lifts one dark, rakish eyebrow. His green eyes are amused. "You doubt my abilities, Kari?"

"Frankly? Yes. As well as my own."

But Charlie's life is on the line. So we *have* to find a way to get this antiwrinkle stuff.

Gustav peers at me intently. "For reasons I will not mention at ze moment, I take zis as a personal . . . how you say? . . . challenge."

"You can take it as whatever you want, but this isn't a game. Those people have my brother, and they're going to hurt him if we don't get them what they want."

Just in case our descriptions are circulated by either the transit guards or the German cop, we change into different disguises. I put on a green wool beret, a French braid that hides the torn section of my hair, a white sweater, and jeans. We put the baseball cap on Gustav, jimmy open his handcuffs, and force him into American-style sweats that he complains are hideous. Matthis gets a ski hat and a puffy jacket with baggy pants that disguise how skinny he is.

After we catch up with Evan (who has "dorked up" in a sweater with rows of dancing holiday reindeer and some pulled-up-practically-to-the-neck corduroy trousers), he arranges for our luggage to be picked up from the little *gasthaus* in Murnau and deposited in two differ- ent train station lockers, even though we've decided to abandon it. It's all too possible that someone—whether it's Charlie's kidnappers, the mystery people who tried to snatch me, or even GI—could have surveillance on the lockers.

The bottom line is that we all have our backpacks with the essentials: phones, laptops, and assorted tricks of the trade. Clothing is easily replaceable, and I have a spare set of travel underwear with me.

In a matter of hours, we've hopped onto different trains for the four-hour journey to Zurich and reassembled in a new hotel room, this one at a Marriott.

Zurich is a stunning, rich, international center of banking and industry that lies on the north shore of a lake, the Zürichsee. The river Limmat flows through it, and Old Town is to the west.

We're starving when we arrive, but we don't want to take the chance of being seen together as a group, so Evan and I go out alone in search of pastries.

Upon our return I open the hotel room door to find Gustav examining one of my bra-and-panty sets, which I left zipped inside a compartment of my backpack, thank you very much.

"What in the hell do you think you're doing?" Evan demands before I can even close my gaping mouth.

Gustav's dirty smile flickers over the cleft in his chin. His green eyes dance at the annoyance in Evan's tone. "Reconnaissance?"

I march over and snatch the panties out of his hand. They're purple and lacy and probably wickedly expensive—I don't know for sure. Why? Because Evan bought them for me at Victoria's Secret months ago in

Washington, in the course of a different mission. It's a long story—and it doesn't mean a thing. There's nothing between us.

I scoop the bra off the bed. Then I stuff both items into my backpack, where they belong. "What gives you the right to go through my things, pervert?" I cast a glance of reproach at Matthis, too, for allowing this to happen.

Matthis gives me a helpless, how-was-I-supposed-to-stop-him? expression.

"I am no pervert!" Gustav exclaims. "I merely like to know wis whom I am working, eh?"

"That's usually accomplished through conversation, not panty raids," Evan says.

"I must protest my innocence!" Gustav lays a hand over his heart. "This was no raid. I look only for a pen. . . ."

"Really?" I ask. I open the shallow drawer of the sleek, modern desk in the room, extract a ball-point pen emblazoned with the hotel's name and website, and toss it at him.

He catches it left-handed and has the grace to look a little shamefaced, but not for long. "Ah, Kari—forgive me. You must understand, you are a beautiful girl, eh? I wished to know more about you. Is thees such a crime?" His green eyes are now soulful.

Evan makes a disgusted noise in the back of his throat.

Okay, okay . . . so it's definitely a little disturbing to find a hot French guy burgling your panties. But . . . oh, how to explain the effect Gustav has on me, and probably on most girls? He's enigmatic and charismatic. He's a bona fide thief—sue me, but that's sexy. He's got that whole five-o'clock shadow thing going. He's outrageous but charming. And that French accent of his is growing on me.

Not to mention the fact that he tells me I'm beautiful. How many girls are immune to that? It's not a totally unpleasant thing to hear.

"You will forgive me, eh?" Without warning, he snatches my hand and kisses it. The wicked twinkle has returned to his eyes. "Please, my Kari?"

Here's the thing: I know I'm being manipulated shamelessly. I get that. And Gustav knows I know it . . . and he's highly entertained by the fact that I can't stay mad at him.

Evan, on the other hand, is not amused. "She's not 'your' Kari. Get up, you tosser. And please, for the love of God, would you shave?"

Gustav ignores him.

I try to free my hand, but he's not ready to relinquish it yet. While he doesn't know my skill set and I could knock him out cold within two seconds, I can't help but think this reaction might be extreme. So I decide to flirt with him just a little—not that I know how, but I may as well give it a try.

"I'll, uh, never wash this hand again," I say awkwardly, then cringe at what a stupid line it is. Couldn't I have come up with anything better?

"*Vraiment?*" He gets to his feet and gazes down at me.

I shift uncomfortably. "Heh." I tug on my hand again, but to no avail.

"*J'adore* your lingerie," Gustav murmurs. "Violet. Ze color of passion." He's being totally over-the-top, knows it, and doesn't care.

"Ha!" I'm so uncomfortable and out of my element that I pig-snort. I'm trying for sophisticated banter here. *Trying.* "Yeah. So maybe you should show me yours."

As soon as the words are out of my mouth, I cringe. *Stupid, stupid, stupid!*

Gustav's green eyes smolder. At least I think that's what eyes look like when they smolder—I'm no expert. "Show you my what, Kari?" he asks softly.

"Bah ha!" I jerk my hand out of his as if burned. "So, pastries, anyone?" I turn and root through the bakery bag.

Once the crackling of the paper has subsided, I realize that there is dead silence in the room. Cautiously, I look up from a brioche—it's either that or a croissant I'm going to inhale—and find Matthis evaluating me as if I'm a science experiment gone wrong. Evan's face is like thunder. And Gustav is smirking at both of them.

"Uh." I laugh like a small donkey. "*Pain au chocolat?* Danish? Streudel?"

Evan walks into the bathroom and slams the door.

Matthis falls on a Danish as if he's a starving zombie and it's a plump, freshly torn-off human arm.

And I'm left standing there, looking anywhere but at Gustav, who is chuckling now at my expense. I can't even duck into the bathroom to hide, because Evan's cut off that option. So I opt to shove the entire brioche into my mouth, in hopes of camouflaging my flaming face. Flirting? Not part of my repertoire. I clearly *suck* at flirting.

Let's hope I'm better at high-stakes corporate espionage and grand larceny.

Chapter Twelve

"Of course I will accompany you on ze stakeout," Gustav says to Evan. "I already know ze Jolie building and some of ze schematics."

"No," Evan says dismissively. He stares down at Gustav from his superior height. "You will not. Kari and I will go alone. You will stay here and work with Matthis on *all* of the schematics . . . and if you can get your felonious paws on a blueprint of the laboratory wing, in particular, it would be helpful."

"I am not a minion," Gustav declares. "I will not be ordered, eh?"

"We're all Evan's minions," I say drily.

"You'll bloody well stay in the hotel," Evan tells him. "Or have you forgotten that your face is plastered all over the telly?"

"Baht—" Gustav breaks off, nonplussed. "Oh."

"Yeah. Oh." Evan points at his hair. "And if you've got any sense in that Gallic skull of yours, you will tint your hair white blond and bloody-well shave that Euro-scruff off your disgustingly dimpled chin."

"It's a cleft," I correct him.

"What?" Evan swings around.

"Not a dimple."

Silence.

I shrug. "Just saying."

Evan glares at me.

"Who pissed in his Cheerios?" Matthis mutters to me.

I shrug again. Evan has been in a sour mood since we arrived yesterday. I wonder why? No telling. I gather my things together.

My things include Matthis's video sunglasses, a key fob that's a code scanner, and a cute little set of lock-picks that my dad gave me for my thirteenth birthday. I also have a 4.5 million-volt stun gun that looks exactly like a pink, girlie cell phone. It will drop a charging bull.

I may have zero ambition to be a spy, but as the daughter of two of them, I've gotten to play with some cool gadgets. Rita, who does want to be a spy, unearths new ones all the time. She is not-so-secretly envious that I'm in Paris at GI and she's stuck back at Kennedy Prep in Washington, DC.

Rita's also rebelling against the six-month moratorium on technology that her parents slapped on her. I know she's on Kale's computer and iPad every chance she gets. Her parents, Senator and Mrs. Jordan, are so busy and so clueless that they haven't figured it out.

The Zurich headquarters of Jolie, Inc. are huge, modern, and beautifully designed. The six-story white building stretches an entire city block, and to either side of the main entrance rises a giant decorative structure that reminds me of a Matisse paper cutout. The effect is airy, artsy, whimsical, and elegant.

We hoped initially that we might be able to blend in with some of the employees and walk in, but that's not going to happen. Every worker wears a scannable ID badge around his or her neck, with a photo on it, and goes through security on the way in and out. My guess is that the company's founders are extremely protective of their innovative technology and wary of competitors—not to mention corporate spies. And they should be; Jolie, Inc. is a leading worldwide brand worth billions of dollars.

Evan and I must be aware that while we're doing surveillance, Jolie, Inc. is surveilling us. There are cameras everywhere. So we don't want to be loitering on the street. Across from Jolie is a hotel with a café/bar on the ground floor. We take a table there and order cappuccinos.

Evan takes our task seriously, as do I, but he still seems moody and he's not at all talkative. I put up with this for about half an hour, until I finally get exasperated.

"Why are you so cranky?" I ask him.

"I don't know what you're talking about." He takes a sip of his coffee, keeping his eyes on a newspaper in front of him.

"Yes, you do." I shiver in the chilly December air and fill my mouth with cappuccino, taking comfort from the heat and slight bitterness as it travels down my throat. Evan's expression is neutral and professional, as if I'm some stranger he happens to be sharing a table with. It's an expression that sets my teeth on edge—as if I've turned on the television to a familiar channel and am getting nothing but "snow."

Across the street, a limousine pulls up to the Jolie headquarters. A uniformed chauffeur gets out and opens the door for a party of four très chic, important-looking people—an older woman, a twenty-something woman, and two middle-aged men.

"Valerie d'Haussonville, founder of Jolie, and her granddaughter CoCo," I tell Evan, reading from my phone. Rita has been up to her old hacking tricks and is providing a wealth of information. "The two suits are the COO and the in-house counsel."

"Great. That doesn't help us get inside," Evan comments.

"Rita says they're here for a very high-level meeting; the unveiling of an important new antiaging product. And that product may just contain the ingredient we need. She's doing her best to hack into Madame d'Haussonville's e-mails, but they're password protected and heavily encrypted."

"Encryption usually doesn't stop Rita," Evan muses. "As for the password, does she still have that Backtrack software? The program she was going to use to get into Mr. Carson's laptop?"

"I'm sure she does." My attention wanders from the Jolie building. Mr. Carson is not my biggest fan. He happens to be the director of the Agency my parents double-crossed . . . and Luke's dad. Mr. C is probably thrilled that his son will be taking Tessa Wellington to that dance. Almost as thrilled as he is that I'm thousands of miles away from Luke.

So is Luke my boyfriend—or is he my ex-boyfriend now? He hasn't called me back to say. Go figure.

A steady stream of traffic whizzes by. The air gets colder; so does my coffee. We're going to have to move on soon; nobody stays in a café all day long. Before we do that, however, we need to plant a couple of small cameras. We'll let those do the work for us in the next few hours, as we return to the hotel. Then we'll disguise ourselves and return here this evening after dark.

We affix one tiny camera to a table leg and another to a black wrought-iron lamppost. We pay our bill and fade into the pedestrian street traffic.

On Skype later, Rita is triumphant. She wears red-and-black rectangular Marc Jacobs glasses that make her look like the editor of some fashion magazine. She's clad in head-to-toe black, from her turtleneck and leather jacket down to her leggings and pointy-toed, criminally expensive Prada boots. She wears a spiky ponytail pulled high on her head.

"I know how to get inside Jolie!" she says, almost vibrating with excitement.

Kale waves. He's sprawled full-length on the ugly plaid couch behind her, his arm draped around her waist as she sits on the edge. They're in the living room of his dad's apartment in DC.

Evan, Matthis, and I are grouped around Evan's

computer at the desk in the hotel room, me in the middle. We all exchange glances. We've had zero ideas, if you don't count driving a Range Rover straight through the front doors of Jolie, Inc., which is not exactly subtle. "You do?" I ask Rita.

Gustav is not part of this little electronic powwow because he's in the shower—singing. Very badly.

"They take interns!" Rita announces. "Year-round. And guess who's looking to intern abroad over the winter break, to brush up on my French and German? And guess whose mom actually *knows* Madame d'Haussonville from the international charity circuit?"

We all exchange looks again. I may have mentioned that Rita's parents are Senator and Mrs. Jordan, who are very influential and very social. It's not so surprising that Mrs. J has these connections.

"So guess what?!" Rita jumps up from Kale's ugly plaid sofa and does some kind of dance move—one unknown to me. The cha-cha? Her ponytail develops a life of its own. Kale stares at her gyrating butt. Guess he can't help himself.

"What?" I ask.

"I'm flying out this evening, girl!"

"Huh? Flying out to where?"

"Zurich, dimwit. For an interview. At Jolie, Inc."

It takes me a couple of seconds to process this. "Oh, my God! That's *awesome*."

"I know." Rita preens. Then she wrinkles her forehead. "What is that *noise*?"

Gustav is still strangling two or three cats in the shower. "Uh, you don't want to know."

"Is someone *singing?*"

Evan gives a short bark of laughter. "I wouldn't call it that."

I'm doing my level best to tune out the caterwauling. "So back to our issue: You can literally walk right in the door of Jolie. . . ."

"Yep. And I'll probably be taken on a tour of the whole premises, including the laboratories."

Evan folds his arms across his chest. "It's the best option we have so far," he says, sort of grudgingly.

"Damn straight," I tell him. I turn back to the computer screen and Rita. "You're a genius."

"Well, yeah." She tosses her ponytail.

"When does your flight get in? What airline are you taking?" The singing mercifully stops, thank God. The bathroom door opens and a cloud of steam rolls out.

"Um, I'm not sure."

"But you said—"

"I know, I know. I'm still figuring it out. Don't worry about the details, okay? I'll text you my arrival time in Zurich. And it will be sometime tomorrow. I promise."

"But—"

"Hey, Kari?" She sounds a little alarmed. "Why is there a wet, naked, strange guy next to you?"

I turn my head. Matthis has shrunk away and gone back to his own computer. Gustav is, in fact, still dripping, though to my relief he's not entirely nude. There's a towel riding low on his hips and the trademark smutty grin playing around his mouth.

"And who ees thees?" he asks in his heavily accented English. He gives Rita a slow, thorough once-over and raises an eyebrow.

Rita's mouth forms a silent O.

Kale frowns and sits up, squinting at the computer screen.

"Rita, may I introduce Gustav-the-thief? And Kale, her boyfriend. Who is a *black belt* in karate." I include this friendly warning. "Gustav, this is Rita, our computer genius."

Matthis's head comes up; his expression is a little wounded.

"Excuse me," I amend. "Our *other* computer genius."

Matthis smiles, then looks back down. Everyone has an ego, even the shy among us. "I've got the blueprints to the building," he says softly.

"You do?!"

"Yeah. I tracked down the architects who built the Jolie headquarters. And hacked into their files."

"Well done, Matthis." Evan gets up, then claps him on one shoulder, while Gustav saunters up to peer over the other one, his hair dripping onto the keyboard.

Me, I just hope that the knot in his towel is secure. I don't want to see any more of Gustav than I do already. Not that it's a bad view . . . his arms are nicely muscled and his chest is broad, sprinkled only lightly with dark hair—

"Would you get dressed, you loathsome frog?" Evan asks pointedly.

Gustav's eyebrows shoot up to his hairline. Then he makes a derisive noise. "Bah. I would rather be loathsome than *English*," he retorts.

It's another pig-snort moment for me.

Kale's lips twitch, and Rita laughs. "Well, I've gotta fly! Need to pack. Can't wait to see you!" And she waves good-bye. Then the two of them are gone.

I close the laptop and we all look at each other.

"This is fantastic," I say to Evan and Matthis. "Because, short of hiring SEAL team six to launch a commando raid on Jolie, we were out of options. But I have to wonder how Rita's managing to get a last-minute plane ticket, leaving tonight? And she's very mysterious about it."

Evan shrugs. "The Jordans may have a private plane."

I stare at him. "No, I don't think so. They're rich, but not *that* rich. And even if they do have a plane, it's not like they'd just hand it over to their daughter. . . ."

He eyes me blandly. "Well, it sounds as if she's got a ride somehow. Do you think she'll bring Kale? Maybe even Luke, if the Gulfstream is roomy enough?"

"Luke? Huh?" I shake my head.

"Don't you miss him?"

I shrug. "It doesn't matter if I miss him or not. I'm telling you, there's no jet."

"Whatever you say, darling." Evan yawns and stretches his arms over his head, lacing his fingers together and leaning back. He glances at his watch. "I think I'll take a nap for an hour or so, before we head back for more surveillance on Jolie."

I'm truly mystified about how Rita's getting here.

Last-minute international flights can cost thousands of dollars—not to mention that Rita won't fly anything but business class. No riding in economy seats for her . . .

And why would Evan think she'd bring Luke? That's just weird. It's not like she and Luke are good buddies. I wonder again whether Luke and I have or haven't broken up. Maybe I should call him and apologize—but no, I have nothing to apologize for! He's the one taking another girl to a dance.

I banish all thoughts of Luke and focus on the problem at hand again. If Rita can't get here, and I really doubt she can, then there's one logical solution: I will go on the internship interview, impersonating her. I'll need a crash course in the biochemistry of cosmetics—but we can do that over the Internet.

My hands start to shake yet again as I think about calmly walking into Jolie, Inc. and stealing this stuff from their laboratory. What if I can't? What if I get caught?

I curl my hands into fists. I can't get caught. It's as simple as that. Because failure is not an option. Charlie's life is on the line.

I close my eyes and do my very best to send him reassurance, somehow. Through brain waves, or the power of love, or some kind of magic—I'm not picky about the method. *I love you, Charlie. Don't lose hope. I'm going to get you back.*

Chapter Thirteen

We've had a long night of yawning surveillance at Jolie, Inc. when the weak winter sun comes up. All it tells us is that there are two daily shift changes and no night staff, though there are janitors who come in the early evening and armed guards patrolling the perimeter of the building all night. The security system is primo. The only way into the place is by invitation. Even Gustav is impressed, and he's dismantled not only the security systems of more than one large museum, but the one at Jolie's own Munich branch.

"Zut alors," he says, shaking his head. *"Je ne c'est pas."*

We go back to the hotel, where he and Evan watch a twenty-four-hour news channel on TV and Matthis loses himself once more in the blueprints, focusing on the laboratory side.

I chug coffee while trying to educate myself about

botanical biotechnologies on the websites of various cosmetics companies—particularly Jolie's.

"Did you know," I say casually to the guys, "that Jolie started their biotechnology unit in the French countryside after they got the idea to take stem cell cultures from roses? They obtained some kind of extract from the cultures that helps with skin regeneration."

I get a couple of man-grunts in response.

"And they derived another product from xylose, which they got from beech wood, of all things." Who knew? I'm fascinated, despite not being a big science buff. So I keep reading. I figure I'll need to be able to chatter about this stuff when I go on the interview at Jolie. Rita's going to text us soon with the day and time—it could be as early as this afternoon.

"Wow . . . over the years, they've developed this product called Revive to the point where it works as well on aging skin as laser treatments. That's pretty cool. . . ."

Despite my real interest, my head is throbbing from too little sleep and too much caffeine, so I close my eyes and lean back in the too-comfy armchair for just a second, or so I think. . . .

I'm jolted awake by a firm knock on our hotel room door. Evan gets up to open it, and in walks Rita, followed by Kale. I'm positive that I'm dreaming. I must be.

"Hey, kids!" she says. "Wake up!" Rita looks as if she just stepped out of *In Style* magazine. She's wearing the same red-and-black glasses, but she's changed her spike-heeled boots for short, flat biker ones more suitable for travel. Her jeans are ripped to the point that they show a lot of smooth dark skin, even in this brutal cold.

She sports very little makeup, but her lips are a fla-grant, stop-sign red—the same red that's in the glasses, of course. And she's wearing my favorite mismatched ear-rings: one diamond stud filched from her mom's jewelry box, and one long, dangly silver handcuff. Rita always makes a fashion statement and always carries it off beau-tifully. I'm not sure how she does it—I would look like an idiot if I tried to wear some of the same things.

Gustav takes her in from head to toe and then zeroes in, with laser focus, on the exposed skin showing through her jeans. "Bonjour, Rita!" he says with his dirty smile.

"Bonjour, Gustav."

"*Enchanté*," he says, clasping her hand. He's about to raise it to his lips when Kale steps into his space and holds out a large paw.

"Duvernay." He nods.

At least he didn't pee on Rita's leg to mark his terri-tory, but this is pretty close.

"Inoue." Gustav frowns and eyes him with far less interest than he did Rita. Finally he drops her hand, takes Kale's, and shakes it. "You, I am not quite as delighted to meet, but zen, you are not as . . . how you say? Cute." He delivers this line with a wink at Rita.

She giggles.

Kale only gives him a cool stare.

Evan says, "Gustav, don't you have something better to do than flirt?"

He takes a moment to think about it and rubs at the scruff on his chin that Evan so despises, then grins. "*Mais, non.*"

"Are you guys actually here?" I struggle out from under my laptop and stand up.

"Yes! Can you believe it?" Rita gives me an exuberant hug. She smells faintly of Joy perfume (her mom's) and, weirdly, peanuts. Maybe from the plane.

I turn to Kale, who I swear is taller—and broader—than the last time I saw him. Is that possible? He's got dark circles under his eyes, and he looks a lot more rumpled than Rita in his plain Levi's and gray hoodie sweat-shirt. He gives me his sweet, low-key smile and holds open his arms. "Hey, Mighty Mouse," he says. "Good to see you."

I step into them and am instantly locked in a cage of human muscle. Kale and I have taken martial arts classes together for years. He calls me Mighty Mouse after an old cartoon series that his dad showed him. It features a mouse as Superman, and he says I remind him of the character because I'm small but lethal in karate.

Kale himself isn't that tall—only five feet eight inches—but he is rock solid. I'm not kidding, the guy could bench-press a Volkswagen.

"I can't believe you guys are here!" I exclaim. "How? Those last-minute tickets are crazy expensive. . . ."

Rita shrugs this off. "What matters is that we made it," she says. "Right, Kale?"

He nods.

They greet Evan next, and then Matthis, whom they only know from Skype.

"So." Rita reaches up and tightens her ponytail, then cracks her neck. "My interview is in less than five hours, so we really need to get a game plan together."

I open, then close my mouth. "Well, but . . . I thought that I'd go . . . you know, as you. I've been doing research on cosmetic biotech companies and memorizing phrases like 'the architecture of skin tissue' and 'jasmonic acid derivate.'"

Rita takes off her glasses and peers at me while she cleans them on her shirttail. "No way. I'm all about this mission, Kari. You know I love anything to do with style—and that includes cosmetics. I didn't take Honors Biology and second-year chemistry for nothing either. I am actually the perfect candidate to go on this interview. In fact, assuming they don't catch me stealing redhanded, I think I'll do this internship for real!"

I gape at her. "Are you sure?" I cast a sidelong glance at Kale, who looks very unenthusiastic about this plan. But he says nothing.

"Yep." Her expression turns serious. "So . . . I'm almost afraid to ask, but have you heard anything else from the kidnappers? Have they let you talk to Charlie?"

I close my eyes. I've tried to block the sound of Charlie's screaming from my head, but I can still hear it.

"Sorry," Rita says quickly. "Maybe I shouldn't have asked."

"No, it's okay. . . ." I fill her in on the last interaction I had with the mechanical voice, the one with the noise of the band saw in the background.

Evan breaks in. "I think they're just trying to scare you, Kari."

"Yeah? Well, it's working."

"I don't think they're actually going to harm him. The band saw—it was just a tactic."

"Well, they did something to him to make him scream like that!" My voice cracks. "That wasn't just for shits and giggles."

Rita puts her hand on my arm. "Calm down, Kari. Nobody in his right mind could hurt a kid as cute as Charlie."

"Who says these people are in their right minds? We have no idea! What kind of weirdo wants an ingredient from a cosmetics company? Seriously? What are they planning to do with it?"

She shakes her head. "I don't know."

"Rita, let me be the one to go on the interview," I beg. "We can't screw this up—"

"Wow, Kari. I don't really like the implication here, that I'm not as good as you are."

"I didn't mean it like that. It's just that there's so much at stake here for Charlie—"

"That you'll be twice as nervous as me. Plus, if Mrs. d'Haussonville decides to look in on my interview personally, she will be expecting a half-Indian girl who looks like my mom: in a word, *me*. Larita Jordan. And I have the right background to be a good candidate, plus my French and German are a hundred times better than yours, plus you have all the fashion sense of a scarecrow—"

"Thanks so much," I say, stung, even though I know she's right.

"Truce, ladies." Evan steps in, probably seeing the outrage and hurt on my face. "Kari, let Rita go on the interview. She's not going to be breaking into the laboratory right then and there. Her objective will be something far more simple: to grab security codes with a scanning device, or if at all possible snag an employee's badge. She's up to that. Okay?"

I sit back down in the armchair and draw my knees up to my chest, hugging them tightly. I glare at them moodily. Finally I nod. "But what if they scan fingerprints or something to get into the secure areas?"

Evan looks at Rita. "Then grab someone's coffee mug or tape dispenser on your way out . . . something like that. Even a notepad would probably do. Anything with a surface that a print might adhere to."

She nods. "I can do that. I'll take a big handbag."

Evan nods. "And while you're there, do you suppose you can get us access to the security cameras?"

Rita purses her lips. "If I can just get a moment alone with a security guard's computer, then I can upload a virus to it that will get us into the system later. But it may be tricky."

Matthis lifts his head. "I have an idea on that. . . ."

He's so quiet that it's easy to forget he's in the room with us.

"What's that?" Evan asks.

"Jolie still does some testing of cosmetics on animals, though they have gotten better about it. So if some radical protesters happened to come by and create a ruckus outside, security would be obligated to check it out."

"Brilliant!" Evan smiles for the first time in a couple of days. "Right, then. Gustav, Kale, and I will march for the rights of, ah, pit bulls not to wear lipstick."

"That's actually not funny, Evan," I say. "Product testing on animals is a real issue."

"I stand corrected and suitably chastened. Perhaps we can rescue some when we go into the lab for the secret ingredient."

I evaluate him for any signs that he's patronizing or mocking me, but he seems serious.

While the rest of us keep going over the building schematics and try to troubleshoot, Rita brushes up on some of the cosmetics and biotech stuff I've found at various websites, and then takes a shower to freshen up after traveling all night. She dresses in a sharp black-and-white Chanel jacket she snagged from her mom, a cobalt-blue cashmere sweater, and black trousers with her spike-heeled boots. Her makeup is subtle but expertly applied, and her big, roomy bag is Louis Vuitton.

She drapes a jumble of different necklaces around her neck in a combination I'd never put together—but it looks fabulous. And hidden on one of them, on the back of a semiprecious gem, is a microphone so that we will be able to hear everything she does. In each of her earrings is a small camera that will record every step of her journey inside Jolie, Inc.

She looks impossibly chic but also friendly and approachable, which is hard to pull off—and it's a combination that a major cosmetics company should find irresistible in an intern.

In the meantime, we've sent Evan to an art supply store for paint, brushes, and poster board. Our next step is to create some suitable protest signs for our "animal rights activists." Matthis and Gustav get to work while I research what kind of testing Jolie, Inc. actually does on animals. I figure it's best to know the truth.

Jolie claims to market only cruelty-free products, but has a dirty little secret: China. It recently entered the Chinese market, where the law *requires* testing of products on animals. So Jolie finds that in the name of global expansion, it's caught between a rock and a hard place. Interesting.

It gives our protesters enough of a platform for this afternoon, anyway. While we have no proof that the "testing" they're doing actually harms any animals, we just need to create a brief distraction.

Matthis's best sign reads JOLIE'S ANIMAL TESTING NOT SO PRETTY, and features a model with horrific burns and blisters, holding a bunny with the same. It turns my stomach and gives me even more reason to avoid makeup.

Rita turns a little green at the picture of the poor bunny. "Will you keep that away from me?" she begs. "And when I get back, I'm going to check every single cosmetic I own to make sure it's not tested on animals. . . ."

Evan, Kale, and I will be the animal rights protesters. Accordingly, we put on rubber animal faces held in place by elastic. Kale wears the rat's. Evan makes a terrible bunny, but I refused, so by default I get the dog nose. We camouflage the rest of our faces so we can't be identified and tie or slick our hair back.

We also wear fake fur that we've "bloodied" with red paint, and assorted "blisters" that we've made with paper and dried glue and pink paint.

Finally everything is ready—or as ready as it's going to be.

Evan's asked the hotel to call two taxis, one for Rita and one for me, him, and Kale, the protesters.

Matthis watches from the window as we all get into the cars and drive away. The boys and I ask to be dropped off down the block from Jolie.

Thanks to her earring cameras and a special feed that Matthis has routed to our phones, we see Rita's progress down the Bahnhofstrasse—Zurich's main shopping street—and then east from there. It's the same route that Evan and I took the other morning, and again last night.

After a few more turns, the cab eventually pulls up to the building, and Rita thanks the driver after paying him. Then she straightens her shoulders, takes a deep breath, and says, "Wish me luck."

Chapter Fourteen

Rita is reflected in the glass doors behind the modern architectural "lace" of the building's partitions as she walks into Jolie, Inc. Her shoulders are back, her head is high, and there's a smile on her face that reflects total professionalism. She looks like a winning candidate, someone almost entitled to the internship. I have to admit that she's playing it perfectly so far.

She is stopped just inside the doors by a uniformed guard and a metal detector. She puts her purse on a conveyer belt to go through an X-ray machine, similar to those at airports worldwide, then steps through. The metal detector bleeps.

"My necklace and earrings," she says apologetically in French. "Would you like me to take them off?"

No! The earrings are our only visuals, and the necklace is our audio.

The guard shakes his head, thank God. He scans her visually and passes her through when her purse displays nothing unusual on the monitors. Who would ever think to examine her compact? It certainly doesn't look as if it contains a thumb drive holding a computer virus.

Rita takes her purse back and heads for the reception area. This is all done in white, with screens similar to the architectural ones outside, perforated with Matisse-like cutouts. Here the negative space is utilized to display Jolie products and lit with neon blue. The long counter is done in silver and white. It's all very artistic and modern.

Behind the counter are female employees in impeccably tailored dark suits with white blouses. One of them, a polished blonde with her hair drawn back in a clip, greets Rita in French, rather than German. Evidently the whole company conducts business in French, since the founder is originally from Paris. *"Bonjour, Mademoiselle."*

"Bonjour. Comment allez-vous?" Rita says with a winning smile. "I have an interview at three p.m., with a Monsieur Luttrell."

"Ah, oui. Un moment, s'il vous plait." The woman checks her computer.

"What a beautiful interior," Rita says, switching to English and turning slowly in a circle as if to admire it. We know it's actually for our benefit.

"Merci, mademoiselle. It is a privilege to work here in such surroundings. The design is by a young woman who studied with Frank Gehry."

Since it's still a few minutes before three, she asks Rita to wait and gestures toward a pale green, backless couch shaped like the number 8. Inside the top oval of the 8 grows a ficus tree. Inside the bottom oval is a fountain with peach rose petals floating in it.

It's pretty, but odd. I wonder if someone who works there has to shred a couple of roses daily just for this purpose—and clean out the old ones.

Rita sits down on the couch and checks her watch. "Go," she whispers.

On cue, Kale, Evan, and I burst through the front doors with our graphic signs, chanting, "Jolie: not so pretty! Jolie: not so pretty!" in both French and German. "Stop animal testing!"

"*Zut!*" The guard moves immediately to eject us.

Our plan is for Evan to allow himself to be "overpowered" by the guard while I scream abuse at the poor guy. As this happens, Kale vaults over the conveyer belt and bypasses the metal detector, setting off an alarm. He sprints like a maniac through the reception area of Jolie. He heads toward Rita, who screams and runs away from him, straight for the long silver-and-white counter. He heads after her and vaults over it, too, causing the two employees there to scatter.

Meanwhile, I've allowed the guard to eject me. He turns and heads for Kale. Rita has about five seconds to upload the virus to one of the reception computers. Kale decides to give her a little more time: He springs back up onto the counter and runs along it, shouting and gesturing. Then he does a handspring clean over the guard and runs for the door, the mortified guard in hot pursuit.

Rita, who has hidden behind the counter, finds herself

being comforted by the two reception employees, who rush over to her just as she closes her hand around the flash drive to remove it. Luckily, they're too flustered to notice, and she pretends to just be leaning against the counter.

"*Mademoiselle, je regret*—we are so sorry—are you all right?"

"Oh," says Rita, pretending to be shocked and dazed. "Yes, I think so. I'm fine."

"This is not a usual occurrence, you understand. . . ." Clearly shaken themselves, they try to reassure her.

"That guy is crazy!" she exclaims.

They all commiserate with each other.

Things couldn't have gone any better. Outside, the guard, purple in the face, threatens us and shoos us off the premises while we mock him and ask him how he likes working for bunny killers, etc.

Evan, Kale, and I take up marching in a circle with our signs across the street. Most people ignore us, but a few yell encouragement. I palm my cell phone and watch the feed, while Evan and Kale do the same with theirs.

Inside, Luttrell has appeared and ushers Rita solicitously toward his office for the interview. She continues to play it perfectly, asking for just a moment to powder her nose and compose herself after the unexpected drama.

In the WC, she slides the flash drive back into its groove in her compact, since her purse will have to go through security again on her way out. Then she smooths her hair and clothes before winding her way back through a sea of modern white cubes, past more artistic displays of Jolie products, to M. Luttrell's office.

It's there, with him, that Rita delivers her most impressive performance yet. Evan, Kale, and I listen with raised eyebrows. Rita speaks knowledgeably about "thermal plankton" found in spring water. She talks about it becoming a "cellular collaborator" with keratinocytes, Langerhans cells, and fibroblasts. She demonstrates further knowledge of how it detoxifies the skin . . . and goes on about how exciting she finds other research of Jolie's to be—how it will change women's lives forever.

As she's winding down, Madame d'Haussonville does indeed look in on Rita, wanting to meet her friend's daughter. She finds her charming, of course. And *oui*, of course they will find a spot for her in the intern program!

I restrain a cheer as M. Luttrell agrees wholeheartedly that it seems clear she was born for a position in research and innovation. Rita will join the Jolie family.

There's only one thing left for her to do: snag someone's badge on her way out. Okay, two. She also needs to determine whether biometrics are used to get in and out of the laboratory wing.

Rita is palpably thrilled at winning the internship.

"*Merci beaucoup, Madame d'Haussonville! Et vous, Monsieur Luttrell. Je suis*—oh, I am forgetting my French!—so very excited to have this opportunity. I cannot thank you enough. . . ." She goes on for a while in this vein and then begs for a tour of the premises.

"May I see where the cosmetics are made? I'm especially interested in that!"

Madame d'Haussonville deftly turns her over to a junior public relations employee and bustles off to more important things. Rita makes sure to get her business card and Luttrell's first—so she can write thank-you notes.

Rita moves through the maze that is Jolie, Inc., and we move with her, getting closer and closer to the laboratory wing: the inner sanctum.

It's a good thing that Rita got those business cards, because we will indeed need fingerprints off them to enter the lab section when we return tonight. Matthis will have to figure out a way to transfer the prints to a sheet of film that we can then use to duplicate them.

From the camera on Rita's earrings, we take the tour along with her. The lab wing is the no-nonsense, sterile side of Jolie, Inc. There's no sexy, überchic design here, just white tile floors, stainless steel counters and sinks, and stainless steel refrigerators . . . along with a lot of strange-looking equipment that I wouldn't be able to identify if my life depended on it. I do see something I recognize as a centrifuge, and some petri dishes, but that's about the extent of my knowledge.

Rita keeps up a steady stream of chatter and asks about all the skin-care products on Jolie's website. She's introduced to a small team of scientists in white lab coats. They wear rubber gloves and have goggles hanging around their necks. One's an older guy, and two are women in their thirties or so.

Rita and her earrings begin to eye the badge around one of the women's necks. I can feel her coveting it and trying to figure out a way to get it off her. But there's never an opportunity—even when they both go to the ladies' room at the same time. It would just be too obvious who stole it.

I can almost feel Rita's frustration. Her tour is coming to a close, and she's desperate to get someone's badge—anyone's. The junior public relations employee tries to hurry her along, looking at her watch and making a clucking noise. *"Alors, je regret* but I must be in a marketing meeting in only five minutes! Let me escort you to, ah, how you call it? Human Resources, yes? And they will give you some papers to complete."

Rita thanks her profusely for the tour and says she hopes to see her again soon. They hustle along to HR, coincidentally passing Madame d'Haussonville's office. Rita breaks away to pop her head in and thank her again.

Madame gestures her in and tells her to have a seat. She begins to ask more about how Rita's mother is doing, but the COO stops by and asks Madame to step out into the hallway with him for just a moment. She does, and a short conversation ensues in French.

Rita homes in on the ultimate prize: Madame's own badge, lying draped over her raincoat in a corner chair.

"No!" I hiss, even though she can't hear me.

Rita cranes her head to see the two in the hallway. They are completely oblivious of her.

"Rita, *no*." I'm not even conscious of saying the words out loud.

She smirks. Then casually, she gets up, walks across the room, snags the badge, and stuffs it into her waistband.

Rita smoothly takes three steps to the right, clasps her hands behind her, and pretends to be inspecting the wall of awards that Jolie has garnered as Madame walks back into the room.

I'm holding my breath without realizing it, until Evan pokes me in the ribs and I jump. The air whooshes out of my lungs.

Rita calmly converses with Madame about her mother and her charities and her latest travels, as if she hasn't just committed the ultimate in treachery. It's a little scary, I have to say. I'm feeling guilty that she's taken advantage of this woman's good nature and her friendship with her mom.

I remind myself that the end justifies the means, and the end is Charlie's freedom. Charlie's safety.

Without a blink or any other clue that she has a conscience, Rita accepts two kisses from Madame, one on each cheek, and a bottle of Jolie's latest perfume for her mother. They agree on a starting date for her internship, pending approval from Kennedy Prep back in DC.

"Now, what have I done with my reading glasses?" Madame says with a frown, patting around her neckline and checking on top of her head. "I am always losing things. . . ."

Rita pretends to help her look.

Madame's gaze roams to her raincoat. She lifts it up and checks the pockets while collectively, we hold our breath.

Jesus-God-no-please-don't-let-her-figure-it-out. . . .

"How odd," Madame murmurs. "What—?"

Rita, the ultimate pro, looks totally innocent. She even locates Madame's spectacles for her—they were wedged between two stacks of files and pamphlets on her desk.

And then my friend and coconspirator strides cheerily out the door, spike heels, Louis Vuitton purse, stolen badge, and all.

She's done it!

Chapter Fifteen

Our group gets back to the hotel room before Rita does, so we're waiting when she unlocks the door, strides in, and kicks off her heels. We give her a standing ovation, and she preens, accepting it as her due.

"You were awesome, Rita," I say.

"My badass Bond girl!" Kale grabs her, kisses her on the lips, and then raises her high over his head like a trophy while she squeals.

"Put me down!" Rita orders.

Kale sets her on her feet again. "Your wish is my command."

Then Rita swivels her hips and does a sexy little dance as she slides Madame d'Haussonville's ID badge out of her waistband and dangles it in front of Matthis. He snatches it, dying to create the fake badges.

I have to voice a concern, though, before he gets to

work. "Guys—and Rita—it's unbelievable that we have the company founder's badge, but what if she goes straight to her security team, alerts them that it's missing, and they have this one voided?"

"Well, duh," Rita says, looking unfazed. "Of course that's exactly what will happen."

I stare at her. "So then we're screwed. The badge is useless."

Rita smiles, removes her glasses, and polishes the lenses with a microfiber cloth. "Not true. When I uploaded the virus into Jolie's system, I gained us access to everything, not just the security cameras."

"Brilliant," Evan says.

"Thank you." Rita slips her glasses back onto her nose. "So we'll be able to create two Jolie badges with Gustav's and Evan's photos on them, using the names and codes of two real employees. But we did need a real badge so that we could duplicate the look exactly."

Okay, I feel better now.

"So was I born to be a spy, or what?" She laughs.

I raise my eyebrows. "I just hope Madame d'Haussonville never figures it out."

"She won't," Rita promises.

It still bothers me that Rita doesn't seem to have any conscience about trading on the woman's goodwill this way. . . . I guess it reminds me too much of my double-crossing, double-dipping parents. How could my own mom have pointed a gun at me without even blinking?

Not that I'm implying that Rita'd ever do that—but

let's just say that I trust very few people these days. I need my friends to *have* my back, not stab me in it.

"Isn't it amazing that I got the internship?" Rita says, flopping on one of the beds next to Kale.

One look at Kale's face tells me that he's not at all happy about this. He doesn't want to go back to DC without his girlfriend. Poor Kale. He and Rita used to hate each other, and now he can't live without her.

"Yeah, amazing," Kale says flatly. He refuses to look at her.

"What's wrong?" Rita asks.

"What do you think?" He rolls off the bed and walks to the window, shoving his hands into his pockets while he gazes outside.

"Kale, it won't be for that long."

"Uh-huh."

Rita gives me a helpless look. "Luke and Kari are still dating, even though she lives in Paris. If they can do it, we can. It's just a few weeks."

"Right. And when they offer you a job after graduation? What will you do then?"

"Kale, that's a big assumption—"

"Is it? Mrs. d'Haussonville's your biggest fan now. Why wouldn't she want to hire her friend's daughter?"

"Well—"

"So what would you do, Rita?" he asks in a quietly confrontational tone. "Would you move to Zurich?"

"I don't know."

"You don't know? Wrong answer, brat." I can see

Kale clenching his fists inside his pockets, and it's not a good sign.

"Brat" is what he used to call her, before they started seeing each other. He thought she was a snot. She couldn't stand him either and used to call him "Grease Monkey" because he liked to work on old cars with his dad.

I don't like where this argument is going, and we can't afford for any member of this team to not be focused. Our mission is to get Charlie back, unharmed. It's time for me to become Drill Sergeant Kari.

"That's enough, you two." My voice is a bucket of cold water. "You'll have to get into this later, in private—after we rescue Charlie."

Kale turns his head and fixes me with a hard, resentful stare. "I don't take orders from you, Kari."

"Actually, mate, you do," Evan says, standing up. "We're all in this together, for one reason and one reason only: to get Charlie back alive and in one piece. Our personal issues and emotions have absolutely no place here right now."

As usual, I'm half-annoyed and half-grateful for his interference.

Kale's shoulders tense; he stands like a statue without turning his head again. "We're golden, then, 'cause evidently Rita doesn't have any emotions."

Gustav, silent until now, gives a whistle and walks to the window. He's clearly uncomfortable.

Rita fidgets on the bed; she's uncharacteristically quiet.

I know, and she knows, that if she wants a future with Kale, they've got some major hurdles to overcome. Kale's mom took off on him and his dad when he was really young. He's not going to be happy dating someone who wants to be a spy, always in the field and on the move. But none of this is new, and we cannot afford distractions right now.

"Pull it together, both of you," I say. "I'm sorry, but we need everyone's head in the game here. We're not breaking into a puppet theater tonight. We're breaking into Jolie, Inc. And failure is not an option. We can't screw this up." I stare at everyone in the room. "Do you understand?"

Nobody says anything. The air is thick with tension.

"If the kidnappers send me Charlie's head in a box," I say, "I will not be responsible for my actions."

Everyone focuses intensely on tonight's mission. We pore over the schematics and isolate the one area of the laboratory that seems to have ridiculously over-the-top security. It's an inner sanctum in the inner sanctum, protected by the biometrics fingerprint scanner, then a key-card lock for the safety-glass enclosed room, and finally a stainless steel safe. A safe that Gustav will have to crack.

I don't like the fact that I'm stuck on monitoring duty with Rita and Matthis while Gustav, Evan, and Kale get to go on the heist, but Evan talks me into it.

"We could get caught," he says flatly. "And if that

happens, and you're along with us, then Charlie has no backup team."

I can't really argue with that.

Rita's not pleased to be left behind either, but if she wants to salvage a real internship at Jolie, she cannot be caught on surveillance tape breaking into the building, can she?

Kale grouses about being stuck in the role of getaway driver, but Evan reasons with him. "Like it or not, Kale, you're the muscle. You haven't had the training, and we do need someone on the outside who can take care of any physical threat to us. Preferably someone with a black belt in karate, like yourself. For obvious reasons, we need Gustav inside—he's the expert burglar."

Gustav takes a small bow. He looks quite comfortable in his gray business suit, black dress shirt, and gray-and-black striped tie. Without his customary leer, he looks almost trustworthy.

He and Matthis are content with their roles.

Matthis doesn't want to go; he is a behind-the-scenes guy all the way. Give him a computer or something to engineer, and he's a happy dude.

The badges that Matthis has produced are things of beauty. I doubt that even the head of security at Jolie could tell that they're counterfeit. I guess we're about to find out. I swallow hard and start double-checking things, for about the seventh time.

"Gustav, you got your equipment into place?" For obvious reasons, he can't walk into Jolie carrying a bag of safe-cracking tools.

"Yes, Kari," he answers tolerantly, if somewhat wearily. "As I told you, I stored my case earlier this morning, on ze roof of ze building, eh?"

"But what if someone saw it and removed it?"

"I promise you, zey are not going to find it. It is well—how you say?—camouflaged."

"What if you're unable to get up there? What if one of those rooftop access doors trips a silent alarm?"

Gustav shakes his head and casts a speaking glance at Evan, who reminds me quietly that we've been over all this.

"Kari, Gustav has gotten into and out of museums all over France, Germany, Spain, and Italy—not to mention the Getty, the Boston Museum of Fine Arts, and the Kimball in the States. So he knows what he's doing."

"He was in custody because he got caught red-handed at Jolie's Munich branch!"

Gustav's mouth tightens. "I made a mistake there. But I never make the same mistake twice. I am very, very good at what I do, Kari." His eyes rove lazily over my body. "And I assure you zat I am good at other things too." He winks.

I can't believe he's trying to flirt at a time like this. "You never stop, do you?"

The dirty smile plays over his mouth. "It is part of my charm."

"Is that what you call it?" Evan asks.

Evan, too, is wearing business attire. I'm quite sure that Evan came out of the birth canal in custom-tailored suit and French cuffs, so his new black suit doesn't look at all odd on him, and the glasses he's put on only make him look older and more handsome. But for the first time in all the months I've known him, he seems a little tense. Is it just nerves before the heist? Or something else?

Rita and Matthis get the guys fitted with tiny comm units that attach to the backs of pins on their lapels. Kale's not wearing a suit, so Rita puts his comm unit onto the back of an old silver coin that hangs on a leather cord around his neck. He stares straight ahead, ignoring her as she ties the cord.

Great.

We test the comm units there in the room, and then once again the guys get into the car that we've borrowed from another unsuspecting hotel guest. He or she won't miss it at one a.m.

Before we let the guys go, Rita and Matthis make sure that they have access to the cameras in Jolie's CCTV system.

"Yup," Matthis says. "I got the feed from camera number five pulled up. What about you, Rita?"

Her fingers clatter on the keyboard of her laptop. "Pulling up feed from number nineteen, near the entrance to the lab wing."

"Okay." He stares at his own screen. "Try number eight. Are you seeing—"

"Ugh," Rita says. "Yeah, I'm seeing the guard picking his nose. Next."

"Number three."

"Mercedes S-Class going up ramp into parking garage. Okay, you try number eleven."

"Elevators on second floor."

They go on like this for a while, testing the feed on every single camera. It's crucial that they can freeze and then splice into the feed that the guards see for the few minutes that Gustav and Evan will need to access the lab.

Finally it's time. Gustav and Evan are junior sales executives, returning to the office for presentation materials they've forgotten. We hang their badges around their necks, saying a silent prayer that everything will go well.

I check my watch and make sure that it's synchronized with everyone else's.

Before I let the guys out the door, I have one last thing to say—privately, to Evan. I lean forward and whisper into his ear. "Once you two have the *jungbrunnen*, don't you let Gustav out of your sight—I don't trust him. That stuff must be worth millions of dollars on the black market."

Evan closes his eyes and shakes his head. When he opens them, he flicks my own comm unit with a fingernail. Thunder fills my ears.

Gustav says mournfully, "You accuse me?"

I have forgotten that the comm units are on and working very well.

Mortified, I stand there with my mouth hanging open until Gustav leans forward and covers it with his. He chuckles softly and slips his tongue in between my lips for good measure.

He tastes of espresso, mint, musk, and adrenaline. When he pulls away, his green eyes dance with a peculiar combination of friendly malice and desire. "Wish us *bon chance*, Kari."

Evan's face is like thunder as he shoves Gustav out the door.

Chapter Sixteen

The Jolie building gleams white, cold, and forbidding in the frigid Zurich moonlight. Evan's eyes are now as blank and professional as the dozens of windows that stare down at him and Gustav as they saunter up to the main doors.

Gustav whistles tunelessly as he tugs one open and they walk inside.

The night guard, ever cautious, moves forward to flank them as they scan their ID badges. *"Guten abend,"* he greets them in German.

"Good evening," Gustav replies in English.

The guard switches to English, too. "You are here very late, gentlemen."

Evan nods. *"Zut,* forgot some materials we need for a sales pitch tomorrow."

Gustav lifts an eyebrow. *"He* forgot them."

Evan snorts. "*He* didn't tell me we needed these particular brochures."

"Oh, I need to explain to you how to do your job?" Gustav snipes.

The guard steps back from them. "*Alors*, perhaps you two need a drink." He laughs genially.

"A drink?" Evan says. "That's no cure for his personality problems."

"Ha!" The guard is entertained by them. But it makes me very nervous when he peers closely at Gustav. "I know you from somewhere, eh?"

"I don't think so," Gustav says casually. "But maybe from a party a couple of weeks ago? You have a buddy named . . . Jacques, yes?"

It's a safe gamble. Pretty much everyone in Europe has a friend named Jacques. But I hold my breath and pray this guy doesn't pay too much attention to the news. Specifically, the news about a juvenile thief who escaped from police custody on his way to trial.

"*Jacques*," the guard says, snapping his fingers. "Of course, that's it. Not that I remember so much from that party," he amends sheepishly.

Gustav grins. "Who among us does? Nice to see you again, my friend."

I'm able to breathe normally as he and Evan make their way into the building. They deliberately go to a bank of cubicles in the marketing department on the fourth floor and paw through some poor woman's stuff, though all they actually take before heading back toward the elevators is a department store catalog and a couple of empty manila file folders. Outside the elevators, they make sure to stand and "talk" for a good three minutes or so. This will give Matthis the generic hallway footage he needs to copy for the fake camera feed.

"Okay, Rita—you know what to do," I say. "They're both in the elevator at the fourth floor now. The feed at camera nineteen near the lab entrance needs to show nobody entering, even though the computer will show later that someone did. The camera at the top floor elevator cannot show Gustav getting out—or getting back in with his bag of safe-cracking tools."

"Yes, Kari, I know." Rita's fingers are flying so fast that they look possessed.

"Matthis, you're copying and splicing in the footage from the fourth floor hallway?"

"Yep." He's calm and deliberate, but his tension level is pretty high, just like mine. I know he hasn't slept much lately either.

Matthis squats in typical praying mantis position over his laptop as he does his thing. His eyes behind the blue metallic glasses are beyond intense.

Meanwhile, Gustav shoots to the top floor in the elevator, though somehow Matthis has programmed the buttons at ground level (where the guard is) not to light up and indicate this. I ask him how, but he says apologetically that I wouldn't begin to understand it, so not to worry about it. "Not trying to say you're stupid, Kari," he adds with a sweet smile. "It's just that it's a geek thing."

"Yeah, I know."

I can hear Gustav through the comm unit as the

rooftop door clangs open. His feet crunch on some gravel up there. Then I hear his tools clanking faintly in the bag and more gravel crunching as he walks back. The door clangs behind him. Next I hear an elevator ding.

"Evan?" I whisper.

"Yeah."

"Gustav's on his way down. Don't go into the lab wing until he gets to you."

"Check."

"Houston, we have a problem," Rita says. "There's a regular employee swiping his badge at the front. No telling what floor he's going to."

"Bollocks," says Evan. "Gustav? Duck into the gent's."

"Ze what?"

"WC."

Gustav chuckles. "But I don't like you in zat way, Evan."

Evan says tersely, "Kari, tell us when the coast is clear."

We all wait for what's only a minute or so, while the guy takes the elevator up to the seventh floor, where operations and supply-chain management is. I can't imagine what he'd need there after one a.m., but evidently it's something he can't live without.

"Okay, guys," I say. "You're clear to go to the lab wing. Just hurry. Get in and get that door closed again. You have the prints from Luttrell's card?"

"Yes," Evan's voice reassures me.

Beside me, Matthis smiles with pride. He figured out how to transfer the prints onto a soft, moldable rubber that's almost like Silly Putty. Gustav will pull this over his own thumb before pressing it onto the biometric ID pad.

"You're sure this will work, right?" I nudge Matthis.

He shrugs. "Ninety-eight percent sure."

I can barely watch as Gustav slips the rubber "skin" out of his pocket and tests it out.

Evan swallows hard when it *doesn't* work at first.

I almost pass out.

Rita pinches me, hard.

"Ow! What was that for?" But I don't even listen to the answer, because on the second try, thank God, Luttrell's print finally opens the door to the lab.

"*Apres vous*, Kincaid," Gustav says, his teeth flashing white. And then, when Evan walks past him, "Ladies first."

"I'll kick your arse later," Evan growls. "For now, let's get on with it."

Of course I have a more-than-vested interest in this next part for Charlie's sake. But I'm fascinated from an educational level, too—because I've never seen anyone crack a safe before. So I may actually learn something useful.

"What's in your magic bag, Gustav?" I can't help asking. "A stethoscope?"

He snorts. "That is, how you say? Urban myth. Silly."

"Then what do you have?"

"Curiosity killed *le chat*, Kari."

"The bugger's got a crowbar and a drill," says Evan in dismissive tones.

"Oh, very good, English. I also have an autodialer and a very small ultrasound device—but I will not know what to use until I see ze safe itself."

The lab is dark and full of shadows. As they walk

through, the guys' wing tips make a racket on the tile floors. I don't see any animal cages at all, and I'm relieved about that—though for all I know, there's a top secret bunny room somewhere in the place.

After what seems an eternity, they arrive at a massive safe that is the size of a refrigerator. Gustav sets down his tool bag and evaluates it, stroking his newly naked chin as if he misses his scruff. "Oooooph," he says. *"Putain de merde."*

He sets the bag on a table and unzips it. Then he pulls out a drill and a set of drill bits.

"Gustav!" I hiss. "You can't make that much noise . . . what if a guard hears?"

"Zen we dispose of him," he replies, fitting a very large bit into the drill and tightening it with the key. "Evan, can you please to plug zis in?"

"What, you don't need any more practice bending over?" Evan says. But he does as he's asked.

"*Casses-toi*, eh, English?" Gustav insults him almost affectionately. Then he sets about the task at hand. "Let us hope that zis safe does not have a relocker. I do not think so, because zis is an older model. But—" He shrugs.

The horrific noise of the drill fills our ears, and for far too long. At last, Gustav is finished. *"C'est bon,"* he says with satisfaction, dropping his drill back into the bag. Then he opens the safe. The heavily reinforced door reveals a well-organized space full of vials.

The *jungbrunnen*, a brownish powder, is in the lower left-hand quadrant of the safe.

"How much are we supposed to take?" Gustav asks. He's stroking his chin again, which makes me wonder what's going on in that criminal brain of his.

"Only one vial," Evan says sternly. "One."

"Eh, *bien*," Gustav replies cheerfully. "For my trouble, I take two."

Rita breaks in. "Absolutely not. I have to work there with a guilty conscience already. That stuff has been years in research and development. It's worth millions. One vial only, Gustav."

I'm relieved to hear that Rita feels some remorse.

Our thief rolls his eyes. "*Vous faites chier.*"

"Did you just say we suck?" Matthis mutters indignantly. "And after we broke you out of jail? There's gratitude."

"You broke me out for your own reasons," Gustav reminds us. "And now I have paid my debt." He reaches out a gloved hand and removes a vial, handing it quickly to Evan. "*Bon.* Your precious *jungbrunnen, s'il vous plait.*"

With an odd flick of the wrist, he closes the safe.

And then the shrill, piercing screech of an alarm fills our ears.

"Bloody hell," Evan says, and runs for the exit.

"*Merde, merde, merde,*" says Gustav, and follows.

"What did you do? Did you take more than one? That could have triggered security! Damn it all, I knew we couldn't trust a felonious frog. . . ."

"*Vas te faire fou—*" Gustav pants as he tries to catch up.

"You bloody well took more than one, didn't you?"

"How was I to know?"

"How were you to know? Seriously? Because you're a professional thief, that's how!"

They get to the door of the lab, only to find that the rubber thumb cover won't work this time. Of course not—security has overridden it.

So Evan unzips Gustav's bag of toys, grabs the crowbar, and smashes it into the heavy glass. Nothing.

I'm just about hyperventilating by now.

"Kari, calm down," Rita warns me. "Panic won't do us any good."

"Easy for you to say! Nobody's threatened to send your brother's head to you in a box!"

Evan winds up with the crowbar as if it's a baseball bat and he's Barry Bonds. He's really kind of amazing to watch—especially when this second blow shatters the thick glass of the door. Funny, Gustav doesn't offer Evan the same courtesy on the way out. He dives right through the glass, pulling his bag after him. That's why he doesn't see the guard coming around the corner until it's too late.

"*Arretez-vous!*" the guard shouts.

Right. As if Gustav is going to pay attention to that.

He hurtles forward. So the guard punches him in the jaw and sends him right to the floor.

Good thing Evan comes through the door at him. I get the privilege of seeing Evan's triple-kick sequence—the same one he used on me—and then, naturally, the choke out at the end. Guard-Boy's going to sleep for a while, and for longer than I did. He's not going to feel so good when he wakes up, either.

Evan scrapes Gustav off the floor and tows him along, bitching at him the whole way.

"If you'd just done what you were told, we wouldn't be in this mess!"

Gustav spits something at him that I can't quite make out, but given Rita's gasp, I know is really, really rude.

"I hope that second vial of *jungbrunnen* smashed when that guard knocked you down," Evan continues. "And if it didn't, I'll shove it right up your arse. . . ."

This conversation is interrupted when two more guards come running at them.

Evan immobilizes one with a kick to the solar plexus and then to the left knee. He goes down screaming. The other guard draws his gun and points it right at Gustav.

I'm rigid with fear, can't even take a breath.

Rita pinches me again, which forces me to gulp air. "Snap out of it!" she orders.

Evan takes a split second to evaluate the situation, to decide whether or not to take the risk. Then his foot becomes a blur and the gun flies out of the guard's hand, skittering across the floor. In the same instant Evan chops the poor man in the windpipe, dropping him to the floor.

"Run, Gustav," he orders. *"Run!"*

Gustav does.

Evan stops only to pocket the gun.

Chapter Seventeen

The theft is all over the morning news. A break-in at Jolie is brazen and big-time. Law enforcement is swarming.

While Kale did swap out cars en route back to the hotel, the surveillance cameras caught the license plate of the original "borrowed" car, and the couple who rented it gets hauled unceremoniously out of bed by the Swiss police and put through the third degree. We hear the whole ruckus because it turns out that their room is just down the hall from the two we have. We feel bad for them, but it can't be helped.

Gustav is silent while he plucks glass fragments out of his forearm with Rita's tweezers and drops them into a waiting ashtray. For once he's not trying to flirt with any-one. He knows the whole debacle is his fault—because he did take a second vial. He slipped it down his jacket sleeve when he handed Evan the first one. And of course it broke when the guard knocked him to the floor.

I stare at the remaining small vial of *jungbrunnen* and pray once again for the kidnappers to call. I can't call them—the number that I texted Gustav's photo to has since been disconnected. They're being very careful.

The phone finally rings when I'm in the bathroom, naturally, and I almost run out of there without pulling up my pants.

Evan answers for me. "Hello?" He listens. "Kincaid. Her friend. Here she is." He hands me the phone.

"Charlie?" I ask breathlessly, while buttoning my jeans.

The mechanical voice says, "You have the *jungbrunnen*?"

"Yes. Let me talk to my brother."

"You and Duvernay will head east with it, to Austria. To Salzburg. Just the two of you. Understand? Any others will be shot on sight, and Charlie will pay the price."

"Salzburg," I repeat, nodding even though this person can't see me. "Only Gustav and me."

Evan's eyes narrow, but he says nothing.

"Don't do anything stupid. No police. No Interpol. No nothing. We will call you again in twelve hours."

"I understand. Let me talk to Charlie. Please. I just need to know that he's okay."

There's a pause, and then the voice says, "Fine."

"Kari?" Charlie's voice is high and squeaky.

My knees buckle in relief. I fall onto them, because I am so glad he's alive. I can barely speak. "K-kiddo? You okay?"

"I guess so," he says in a small voice. "Are you coming to get me?"

"*Yes.*" I almost shout the word. "I love you. I'll be there soon."

"Good, 'cuz the food sucks and I hate these people and I'm almost done memorizing the German dictionary and—"

"That's enough," says the mechanical voice. "You know he's alive." It adds ominously, "For now." And then the connection is broken.

I let my body fall forward so that I'm resting on my elbows, my forehead touching the rug. I force myself to take three deep breaths. *He's okay. He's okay. He's okay.*

For now.

"Only you and Gustav?" Evan asks.

"Yes."

He shakes his head. "I don't like it."

"It's probably a trap," says Rita.

Kale runs his hand through his hair. "Of course it is."

"I don't care," I say. "It's my only chance of getting Charlie back. Do you have any better ideas?" I look at everyone in the room, but nobody has a different plan to offer, not even Evan.

"Kari," he begins. He tosses a cuff link from one hand to the other, then back again. "I can't help but think—"

"What?"

"I just—it's a bad idea to meet face-to-face with these people. What if, when they call back, you try to arrange a drop instead?"

"Haven't you figured out that I'm not the one in charge here, Evan?" My voice rises; I can't help it. "These people aren't open to negotiation in any way, shape, or form."

"I think they're bluffing," Evan says.

"Yeah? Well, that's a great theory, Holmes, but I'm not willing to take the chance that they're not. My brother's life is on the line. What don't you get about that?"

Evan takes a deep breath, as if he's about to say something, then stops. "Fine. Never mind. We'll do it the way they've told us to. But it's a guaranteed double-cross, and we've got to be prepared for that."

I nod. "All I care about is getting Charlie out of there. So if it comes down to saving me or him—grab him." I look every one of my friends in the face once again. "Are we all clear on that? Charlie is the priority, no matter what. I've gotten myself out of jams before, and I can again. But he's only seven years old."

Everyone's eyes sort of slide away from mine, which ticks me off. "I'm not kidding. I need you to commit to this, or say you're out. Who's out?"

Silence.

Kale stares into the middle distance at nothing.

Evan folds his arms across his chest, no longer playing with the cuff links.

Rita tightens her ponytail.

Matthis drums his fingers on the lid of his laptop.

Gustav pulls another shard of glass out of his arm and drops it into the ashtray.

"So we're all on the same page?" I ask.

Everyone nods.

"That's better." I know I probably sound like someone's crabby parent, but I can't have anyone squirreling out on me. This is too important.

◇ ◇ ◇

Evan and Gustav are both somber and withdrawn on the five-hour train trip from Zurich to Salzburg. They wear winter hats to hide as much of their faces as possible, and just try to look casual. They don't resemble the two young businessmen whose pictures are being flashed all over the news.

I'm a bundle of nerves again, half-full of anticipation at seeing Charlie and half-full of dread that something will go terribly wrong.

So Kale, Rita, Matthis, and I discreetly try to run through possible double-cross scenarios and how we can survive them. Correction: how Gustav and I can survive them.

Scenario one is that we show up with the vial, hand it over, and both of us get double-tapped: one bullet to the head and one to the heart. I'm not too keen on that one, but where are we going to find bulletproof vests within the next twelve hours?

Scenario two is that we hide the vial somewhere, demand Charlie first, and get tortured until we say where the hiding spot is. *Then* we get double-tapped, along with Charlie. I like this play even less than the first.

In scenario three, Evan, Kale, Rita, and Matthis hide somewhere around the periphery of the meeting spot. They cover Gustav and me with long-range rifles while we hand over the vial and get Charlie. Then everyone walks away happy with no violence, and we never hear from these monsters again.

Of course this is my favorite version, but it's pure

fantasy. We have no long-range rifles, even if I were willing to risk my friends getting shot. Short of robbing a sporting goods store—do they even have guns at sporting goods stores in Europe?—we also have no ability to get rifles in the next twelve hours. Robbing any place is a very bad idea for us, since we're already in the news for two other incidents. Sooner or later, our luck is going to give out, no matter how good we are. It's just the law of averages.

I still cannot understand why the kidnappers want this cosmetic ingredient. It makes no sense to me. I question Gustav about it, and again about who these people could be.

"*Je ne c'est pas,*" he says, shaking his head. But he's avoiding my gaze, and that tells me that he knows more than he's letting on.

"Gustav, you're really pissing me off. At least tell me why they wanted you, of all people, to steal the *jungbrunnen*? Explain that one to me."

"Because . . ." He presses his lips together. "Because they have taken . . . something of mine. So they have, how you say? Leverage with me. They know I will do what they want in order to get zis something back."

"But they needed us to break you out first."

"*Oui.*"

"But why the *jungbrunnen*?"

"I tell you zis already. Zey will sell it to a competitor of Jolie, eh? For a fortune. Raise money for whatever it is that zey want to do."

I think about it. "That's risky, though."

"They're clearly in the business of taking risks," Evan says drily. "Kidnapping is inherently risky. So is extortion and theft. Who knows what else these guys do for fun and profit? A bit of money laundering or human trafficking?"

As soon as the words are out of his mouth, I can tell he regrets them, given my reaction. Bile surges up my throat at the thought of Charlie being sold to some pervert. It's followed by blind panic.

Evan touches my arm. "Kari, forget I said that. I'm sorry." His eyes have gone gray and serious.

"I can't forget it." I rub my damp palms up and down my denim-covered thighs.

"That's not going to happen to Charlie, all right? We're going to get him back."

"Evan, what if they just kill us all?"

He shakes his head.

"You can't be in denial that it could happen. . . ."

"I'm not in denial," he says quietly. "What I'm trying to tell you is that I won't allow it to happen."

"What, you're Superman now? Batman? Spider-Man?" I know I'm being bitchy, but I really can't help it. I don't know how much anxiety and uncertainty I can take; I feel like I'm on the verge of a meltdown.

"Yeah, Kari. I'm all three. I can leap tall buildings in a single bound." He drags his hands down his face. There are deep, bluish hollows under his eyes, and he looks pale. "I'm here to save the day."

I open my mouth to tell him I don't appreciate the sarcasm. "I'm sorry," I say instead. "I don't mean to be so grouchy. It's just—"

"You needn't apologize. If it were my little brother missing, I'd be a raving lunatic. So I think you're doing very well, all things considered."

I look down at my feet—anywhere but at him. I don't know what to do with this kind, understanding side of Evan. When I first met him, he was so obnoxious that I could cheerfully have run him over with a car. And now . . .

Now I don't know.

I stare out the window at the snowy, stunning Austrian countryside. It looks like a panoramic Christmas postcard, with a sky so blue it's almost violet, the mountains in the background, and the evergreens loaded with icicles. It's beautiful, but it makes my heart ache.

Christmas will never be the same. We will never spend it as a family again, with stockings by the fire and eggnog to sip while we sing carols and decorate the tree. We'll never see Dad again in his stupid Santa hat, or eat Mom's spice cookies hot out of the oven, or rip open the dozens of brightly wrapped packages that they've collected for us over the season.

That stuff is a fairy tale now. And I don't care that much about it . . . all I really want for Christmas is Charlie, alive and well and reading *Roget's Thesaurus* page by page, like the adorable little geek that he is.

Chapter Eighteen

Is it appropriate to say that we have to "face the music,"
so to speak, in Salzburg, Austria? Or is that just my dark
humor again? Salzburg is the birthplace of Mozart, host
of the famous Salzburg summer music festival, and one
of the most picturesque cities I've ever seen. Too bad
I'm in no mood to appreciate it.

The massive eleventh-century fortress of Hohensalzburg
looms over the city from the rocks of Festungsberg.
On the left bank of the Salzach River is the Old Town,
where Mozart's home once was. There are also a number
of beautiful old churches there. On the right bank of the
Salzach is the New Town, where Mirabell Palace is, and
the Kapuzinerberg, a steep hill with 250 steps that lead
up to the top and a stunning view of the city.

It's anyone's guess where the kidnappers will want
to do the exchange. We can't imagine that they'll want

to do it in a very public place, but who knows? We take a cab from the train station to the top of an icy hill, twisting and winding crazily around hairpin turns and bumping over cobblestones.

Evan has booked us into a gorgeous five-star hotel—a modernized *castle*—on its own little mountaintop. So that we're out of the public eye, he says. They'll be looking for us in lower-end places.

You think?

When we arrive at the Schloss Mönchstein, I gape like an idiot. I'm glad he's the one paying.

Kale blinks at the snowcapped tower, the vast expanse of snow-covered lawn, the terraces, and balconies. He whistles. "We're staying *here*?"

But Rita strolls in like a queen—and she's warmly greeted like one. The staff couldn't be nicer or more welcoming, and the rooms they give us have breathtaking views of the entire city of Salzburg, with the Salzach River winding through it like a festive silver ribbon.

I take in our surroundings through a fog, because all I can think about is Charlie—and how we're going to deal with the double-cross later.

The weird, mechanically altered voice calls right on schedule, and I jump on the phone, answering on the very first ring. "Hello?"

"You and Duvernay will bring the *jungbrunnen* to the Schiff boathouse along the Salzach, at midnight. You will come alone, as instructed. We will search you both for wires or cameras before the transaction.

If we find either, you will be shot instantly. Do you understand?"

"Will Charlie be in the car?"

"No."

"I want him there. "

"This is not a negotiation." There's a brief pause, and then a shriek from Charlie in the background.

"Stop it! *Stop it!*" I scream. *Oh, God, oh, God.* It's my fault they hurt him. I want to die.

"Midnight," the mechanical voice repeats.

"Yes." My voice cracks. "All right. Don't hurt him again."

"That," the voice says, "is entirely up to you. Try anything stupid, and he dies." With that, the kidnapper cuts the connection, and I'm left staring at the phone with a rising sense of dread.

Gustav doesn't look too happy either. He shakes his head. "I do not like zis."

Evan walks over and gives me a squeeze on the shoulder.

Rita has grabbed Kale's hand and is holding it tightly, her face drawn.

Matthis's lips are clamped together, bloodless.

I know each of them is worried about Charlie—even Gustav, who's never met him.

"Right, then," Evan says, breaking the silence. "I don't think we have much choice in the matter. We can't accompany you. However . . ." He turns to Matthis and nods.

Matthis digs down into a pocket and comes up with

two tiny chips and a tube of superglue. "GPS units," he says by way of explanation. "So that we at least know where you are at all times."

I shake my head. "You heard them. They'll search us."

"We'll attach them somewhere on you where there's already metal," Evan says. He turns to Gustav. "Don't suppose you've got a metal plate in your head, Frog?"

"No, English, I do not." Gustav scowls at him.

"A filling or two in your molars, then?" Evan asks. "Yes . . . ?"

"Then Matthis, you get to play dentist. Glue the chip behind a tooth with a filling. Rita, we'll need those eyebrow tweezers of yours again."

It's hard to say who looks more repulsed—her or Gustav.

"And who will pay my dentist's bill to remove zis chip later?" he demands.

Evan yawns. "I'm sure you can steal something priceless and then pawn it. All in a day's work for you." He turns to me. "Kari? Any fillings?"

I shake my head. I got my dad's teeth, and they're close to perfect, amazingly enough. No braces, no cavities, no fillings.

"Anything metal on you at all?"

"My watch. That's it."

Evan frowns. "Too obvious."

"I know where you can put it," Rita says. "You have underwire in your bra, right?"

Suddenly there are four interested pairs of male eyes

focused on my chest. I feel my ears turning pink, then my neck and face. "Um, yeah."

"Well, they're not going to make you take that off," she points out.

Is it my imagination or do all four pairs of male eyes go a little glassy?

"Brilliant," Evan decides. "Right, then, Kari. Give it to Matthis."

It's Matthis's turn to blush, now. "Uh . . ."

Rita stands up. "Give me the superglue." She gestures to me to follow her into the bathroom, and I do, gladly.

"*Alors*," Gustav announces to nobody in particular, "I would, of a certainty, not need a GPS to find Kari's bra."

Kale chokes.

Matthis stares at the ceiling.

Evan gives Gustav a withering stare.

I ignore him and close the bathroom door on his smutty grin.

It turns out that there's another reason Evan has booked this particular hotel: We don't have to call a cab to go anywhere. A short walk along a winding path through the Monchstein woods leads us higher up the mountain, to a Museum of Modern Art. There's a fabulous restaurant there with more killer views of Salzburg. I look around at spectacular lighting fixtures made of antlers, floor-to-ceiling windows, and colorful contemporary furniture that pops against the white snow on the terrace and the blue-tipped mountain peaks of the Alps.

Under different circumstances, I'd have fallen in love with this place.

We don't do the food justice at dinner because we're all wound so tight, but we have to kill some time, so we sit there and toy with it. Gustav complains that he has to eat with only one side of his mouth because the GPS chip on his tooth feels so odd, and he's afraid he'll somehow dislodge and then swallow it. I can't say that anyone has a huge amount of sympathy for him. He still has a lot to make up for, after what happened at Jolie the other night.

I'm so nervous that I barely swallow two forkfuls all evening, even though the others try to force-feed me. I've been scared before—don't get me wrong. There was a time, a few months back, when I was worried sick about my parents and whether they were alive or not.

This is a whole different level of fear. It's not for me or Gustav. It's for Charlie.

This must be what it's like, sort of, to be a parent. To know that you're responsible for the well-being of a kid who is totally dependent upon you. To know that you'd lay down your own life to keep that kid safe.

When we're done pushing stuff around our plates, Evan pays the check and leads us downstairs in the museum to, of all things, an *elevator* that drops us all the way down the mountain. We emerge from it right on the streets of Old Town.

From there we mingle with the crowds overflowing the holiday markets, and it's surreal to walk past all the stalls and shop windows filled with bread baked in animal shapes; sculpted marzipan; dirndls and lederhosen; rubber duckies in Mozart wigs; miniature violins; carved wooden ornaments; hand-painted beer steins . . . after a while my eyes glaze over and it becomes one big commercial blur. Luckily, it's only a short walk to a café near the river that Evan's found. It's situated not far from the Schiff boathouse on the Salzach.

At ten minutes before midnight, Gustav and I put on our coats, scarves, and gloves. Despite the layers, I feel naked without my usual spy gadgets—I've left them back at the hotel because I know the kidnappers will search us. No lock picks. No scanner device. Worse, no gun.

I feel as if I'm about to face a firing squad. I finger the vial of *jungbrunnen* in my coat pocket and hope that nothing goes wrong.

Rita and Kale hug me. Matthis gives me a two-fingered salute.

I turn to Evan. "Promise me something."

He nods.

"Promise me that if this all goes bad and blows up, you will do whatever it takes to find Charlie and get him back safely." I look up into his gray-blue eyes and fight the weird urge to trace the line of his jaw with my fingers.

His eyes seem to darken for a moment. Then he cups my face between his hands and drops a kiss on my forehead. "I promise."

Gustav and I head out the door of the café, turn

right, and walk along the icy, cobblestoned street. It's freezing cold, but there are still a few other couples and groups of friends out, singing carols, walking home, or moving on to party somewhere else for the evening.

Gustav takes my arm and threads it through his. "At last, I have you to myself," he says with a leer and a waggle of his eyebrows. But it seems forced. I try to play along just to distract myself.

"Um, yeah. At last."

"Ze question is, what to do with you?" He squeezes my hand.

"I have a great idea," I say. "Don't get me killed."

"*Alors*, there is very little romance in a corpse," he agrees, nodding. "So, Kari—"

"Gustav. No offense, but can you not flirt with me, or even speak, right now? I'm about to come unglued."

"Unglued? *Q'est ce c'est?*"

"It's just a figure of speech, Gustav. It means I'm really nervous."

We turn the corner and approach the boathouse. And there, waiting as promised, is the big black Mercedes SUV, windows tinted dark and motor idling. There are two figures in the shadows inside. I wonder if they're the last people I'll ever see on this earth, or if I'm just being paranoid.

The person in the passenger seat is a woman. She opens the door, slides out with one hand in her coat pocket, and says, "Get in." I'm certain that she's holding a gun inside the pocket. She looks familiar . . . where have I seen her before?

"We're not going anywhere with you," I say.

"Get in, or your brother dies."

I clutch Gustav's arm. He eyes me somberly and inclines his head toward the car. We have no choice—he knows it, and I know it.

"Get in!" the woman says, stomping her feet in the cold and clearly losing patience.

Where have I seen her before?

I figure it out as I climb into the backseat of the Mercedes. She was on the Metro platform, that day in Paris when I felt that Charlie and I were being watched. The businesswoman in the navy coat with the yellow scarf. So it wasn't just Lisette Brun watching me.

Gustav climbs reluctantly into the other side; then the woman joins us in the back.

The driver presses the automatic door lock. There's something vaguely familiar about him, too . . . but I don't think I've ever seen him in person before. Maybe I've seen a photo?

My own pulse thunders in my ears. I try to keep my breathing under control, but it's quick and shallow.

"Both of you, untie your scarves and open your coats," the woman orders in English with an accent that I can't place. "Then lift up your shirts."

We comply. It's not every day that I have to expose my half-naked body to two strangers and an oversexed thief, but who cares at this point?

True to form, Gustav gets himself a good eyeful.

Really? At a time like this?

Satisfied that we're not wearing wires, the driver

demands the *jungbrunnen*. I hand it over. He examines it, nods, and pockets it.

"Let me talk to Charlie now," I say.

The woman ignores me and demands our cell phones.

Gustav explains that as he was, up until very recently, a guest of the state, he doesn't have one. She leans over and pats him down just to make sure.

I give her my phone, which she tosses unceremoniously through the window and into the Salzach River. Then she tells me to put my hands behind my back and zip-ties them. She does the same to Gustav. Next, she blindfolds us. I force myself to stay quiet and submit, even though every iota of my body screams to kick her ass. I could knock her unconscious with a single, well-aimed blow from my foot.

I remind myself that it would only get Charlie killed.

Though Gustav has remained outwardly cocky, his breathing has gone quick and shallow, just like mine. So he's as scared as I am. There's something very sinister about these two people.

The Mercedes lurches forward, and we drive for what seems a long time—at least half an hour. We stop at some kind of checkpoint, where the driver speaks German to the guard. It's all I can do to stop from screaming that we're being kidnapped, that these people have my brother, too, and to call the police.

Again, I remind myself that it will only get Charlie killed.

A dank, mossy, almost moldy smell has rolled in through the lowered window. We're near water. The woman opens the back door near Gustav and orders us out of the car, then up a ramp. I hear water lapping and rolling underneath us. We're boarding a ship.

"Where's Charlie?" I demand.

"He's here."

"Then bring him to me. We had a deal."

"Oh, yes. We have a deal, all right," the woman says, her tone heavy with sarcasm.

I stop cold.

"Move!" The woman shoves me.

Now. This is my one moment to make a break for it, before she gets us all the way onboard. We're clearly being double-crossed and taken hostage.

But while I may be able to break free, I can't save Gustav. He'll be shot. And they will kill Charlie, too. I can't take the chance.

With a sense of impending doom, I trudge all the way up the ramp. At the top, someone takes my arm and hustles me across a deck—I can feel wind blowing across my face and through my hair—then into a narrow corridor that leads to some even more narrow metal stairs. We head down, down, and down some more.

I hear an electronic beeping noise that sounds as if someone's unlocking a door.

"Kari!" sobs my brother.

"Charlie?!" I turn my head toward his voice.

Then someone shoves me hard from behind, and I go flying. I collide with my brother, who wraps his arms and then legs around me as I bang into a wall.

I want to hug him tightly—my own little koala bear—as I slide down the wall, into a heap on the floor. But my hands are still zip-tied behind my back.

My jailer cuts the plastic bonds, thank God, then retreats and locks the door behind me.

I throw my arms around Charlie and squeeze him until he squeaks in protest. Tears stream down my face, rolling under the blindfold. "You're okay," I say. "You're *okay*."

"Kari, let go now," he says after a few moments.

"*Are* you okay?" I ask, loosening my grip on him and pushing up the cloth over my eyes.

"You just said I was," he points out with a wobbly grin.

"But *are* you?" I look him over from head to toe. He's grimy and his clothes are dirty; he smells pretty ripe. He looks tired and thin. But he has all his fingers.

"Yeah, I guess so." He peers back at me. "What about you?"

"Sure, Charlie Brown. I'm great." But I look around at the "room" we're in with growing trepidation. I cannot imagine what these cells are used for normally, and I'm not sure I want to know. We're in a box made entirely of five-inch-thick glass. It's transparent and heavily reinforced and evidently soundproof, because we can't hear a thing outside. On the exterior, next to the door, is a lock accessible by a key card.

Inside is a thin, grungy mattress, a wool blanket, and a pillow that is so gross I'm actively afraid of it.

Gustav has been tossed into an identical box right

next to us. He lies still for a couple of minutes, and I'm afraid that maybe he fell when they shoved him and hit his head. I try banging on the box but get no reaction—I don't think he can hear.

There are five glass cells in a row where we are. Across a passageway, there are five more. There's an older gentleman with white hair and a white mustache in one of them. He's got a black eye and some cuts and bruising along his unshaven jaw. He's sitting slumped against the back wall of his cube. His clothes—tweed jacket, white shirt, dark trousers, good leather shoes— are expensive, but like Charlie, he looks as if he hasn't had a shower in days.

Gustav finally sits up, pushes off his blindfold, and looks around. He sees us and lifts a clearly discouraged hand in greeting. I do the same.

"Who's that?" Charlie asks.

"Gustav. He's . . . a friend. He came with me to get you out."

"Oh." Charlie grimaces. "Guess that didn't work so well."

My brother is the master of understatement.

Gustav peers across the passage. The moment he sees the old gentleman, he jumps to his feet and starts banging on the glass like a wild orangutan.

The old dude finally turns his head, peers at Gustav, and jumps up, waving wildly. Tears roll down his cheeks, and he presses his hands and forehead against his own box. These two clearly know each other—and in fact, Gustav resembles him. Same eyes. Same cheekbones.

Gustav "walks" the walls and ceiling of his glass cube with his hands, every inch, probably to see if he can find any sign of weakness. There is none. Dispirited, he drops to the floor again, looks at us, and raises his hands, palms up, clearly saying wordlessly, "What do we do now?"

I wish I knew.

Chapter Nineteen

Gustav and I try to develop a way of communicating silently through the glass, but between the language barrier and the sound barrier, it's tough.

He points at my brother and mouths, "Charlie?"

I nod. Then I point at the older gentleman with a questioning look.

It takes a while, but I finally understand that it's Gustav's grandfather who's in the cell across from us—and now it makes sense that Gustav was so willing to help these monsters steal the *jungbrunnen*. Like me, he had no choice: A family member's life was at stake.

The glass cells are virtually airless. They're also smelly and humiliating—the bathroom facilities consist of a sturdy bucket and a roll of rough paper towels. Fortunately, Charlie stands in front of me and shields me when I have to use the bucket.

The ship rolls back and forth—not dramatically, since it's a big enough vessel—but enough to make me nauseous. I really hope I don't have to puke in that bucket of fun on top of everything else.

A guard wearing a ski mask comes to deliver basic meals: a tasteless, runny stew of mystery meat, potatoes, and carrots; some bread; and two bottles of water.

"Who are you guys? Why are you holding us?" I ask him.

He totally ignores me.

"How long are you going to keep us here?" I try again. Nothing.

Gustav and his grandfather mime back and forth, but I have no idea what they're saying. It's hard to read lips in English, much less in French, and their hand gestures make no sense to me. Charlie doesn't understand either.

Twenty-four hours have passed, with nothing more than another bad meal—chicken smothered in a brown sauce—and an additional blanket. I use it to cover the scary pillow while Charlie spoons against me and we try to sleep.

"Kari?" he says before drifting off.

"Hmmm?"

"This still sucks, but I'm not as scared now that you're here."

"Me either, Charlie Brown. I was terrified when those guys made you scream on the phone." I can't bring myself to ask what they did to him. I don't know if I can handle it.

"They pulled my hair really hard and almost chopped

off my fingers with garden shears," he says in a small voice. He snuggles closer.

I hug him, trying to hold back my fury. "I'm so sorry." I tell myself silently that they could have done much worse. But I'm in a rage at how they've treated him. And I still don't understand *why*. And why we're imprisoned. Imprisoned is better than dead, though.

"It's not your fault," Charlie murmurs. Then he adds, "I bit one of them. Hard."

"Did you? Good for you." I stroke his hair and listen while his breathing deepens and slows. I probably shouldn't encourage violence in my little brother, but in this case I think the circumstances require it.

About seven hours later, I startle awake from a fitful sleep. The lights blaze on, and the guards shove two blindfolded people into the room. Two people I never wanted to see again: Cal and Irina Andrews. My parents.

It sounds melodramatic, but my heart stops. My whole body freezes. I just lie there, paralyzed, my eyes fixed on them. I don't know what I feel. Shock? Revulsion? Anger? Hurt? All of the above?

In my last clear memory of my mother, she's got a gun trained on me. I will never forget it, and I'll never get over it.

They're arguing with the guards, but of course we can't hear a word. My mother hands over a list of some kind. She hasn't seen us yet. And suddenly I know with cold clarity *exactly* how I feel.

My parents are the reason that we are in this mess. It's a given.

As former spies for the Agency, they have lied, cheated, stolen, and quite possibly killed people. They've made enemies all over the world . . . and it looks like they've double-crossed the wrong people. There's no other explanation for why we're here.

I'm shaking because I can't contain my rage.

The guards remove their blindfolds, and my dad notices us first—he grabs Mom's arm and points to our cell. She turns, and the expression on her face is one of classic motherly love and concern—but she's a great actress. I know that now. She takes two steps toward our glass cage.

I spit. Yes, it's gross. But nothing else will communicate my disgust for her right now. So I hock up a big loogie and shoot it right at the glass wall of the cube.

Mom and I stare at each other as it slowly drips down. Her face has gone ashen, and she's shaking her head, saying something to my father.

My father has the nerve—the nerve!—to look disappointed in me. This, from the guy who walked out the door on me and Charlie, who boarded a flight to Russia without looking back. This, from the man who left his kids to the foster-care system. He has no right to be disappointed in me. None.

Dad rubs at a scar on his hand. Charlie bit him as well, during that last happy family reunion. And he deserved it.

Beside me, Charlie spits, too.

Dad closes his eyes and drags a hand down his face. He looks at Mom, whose expression is devastated, then takes her hand and squeezes. That's their last moment together, though, because the guards, who've been on their comm units, drag them each separately to empty cubes.

The doors slam on them, and we're all left to stare at one another. Or look away, which is what I do. I turn my back on them. I don't want to see parts of us in them: my dark hair, from my mom, though hers is cut shorter and styled nicely. My eyes, though hers are expertly made up. My dad's angular jaw and the strawberry blond hair and brown eyes that Charlie inherited.

I want no part of these people, and I'm still afraid, somehow, that they've infected me with their immorality. Their treason.

Next to me, Charlie can't help himself. He swivels to look at Mom. "Mom wants you to turn around," he says. "She's trying to sign something to us."

"I don't care."

"But—"

"Don't even look at her, kiddo. She's poison."

"I think it might be important."

I shake my head. "No. She's trying to manipulate us. Ignore her."

"O-kaay . . . ," Charlie says. He turns his back on her again.

We sit for maybe half an hour. Then a weird crackling noise comes from one corner of our box. I peer up at it and see a small, camouflaged speaker that I didn't notice before.

"Welcome aboard, Andrews family," says a smarmy American voice. It's male and sounds like a used-car salesman's. "And of course, young Mister Duvernay."

I exchange a glance with Charlie. Are we supposed to respond to this jerk? Can he hear us?

"Welcome aboard the USS *Revenge*," he continues.

I *so* don't like the sound of that. . . .

"Thank you for the, uh, hostess gifts you brought." The voice chuckles. "Those pass-codes to the Agency headquarters will come in very handy, Cal and Irine. Too bad I can't give you Charlie in return for them after all."

Oh, God. I put my arms around my brother and tuck his head under my chin. Slowly, I turn my head toward my parents. This doesn't redeem them, because we wouldn't be here if not for them. I'm still sure of that. But it explains why they're here. They did try to rescue Charlie, same as me.

The smarmy voice goes on. "And the *jungbrunnen*— well, you kids are smart. I assume you've been wondering about that. A rival . . . colleague, shall we say? Yes, a rival colleague has been using Jolie to move a very rare and highly combustible agent through their face powder. No drug-sniffing dogs, no surprise security checks— perfect! So simple. It's all been almost too easy, I have to tell you. And a quarter teaspoon of this stuff, mixed with another ingredient that for obvious reasons I won't share with you, packs the power of about a hundred sticks of dynamite."

Oh. My. God. These people are terrorists.

And we've unknowingly helped them in their plans for an attack on the Agency.

I stare, horrified, at Gustav. The blood has drained

from his face as he's realized how we've been used.

Besides its explosive nature, I wonder just how toxic this substance is—the *jungbrunnen*—considering that a vial broke and the powder scattered not only across his bare arm, but into the cuts from the broken glass vial. He must be wondering the same thing.

Gustav fixes a long, agonized gaze on his grandfather. Then he draws up his legs, clasps his arms around them, and rests his forehead on his knees.

I can feel his anguish. I wonder to myself what choice I'd make if I had to steal the *jungbrunnen* personally all over again, but knowing what it was and what it would be used for. If that was the only way to rescue Charlie . . . make sure he wasn't tortured. What would I do?

I can't even think about it, much less answer the question. It's too awful.

Charlie, still tucked against me, begins to tremble. "Kari?"

"Yeah, kiddo?"

"They're not going to let us go, are they." He says it as a statement of fact, not a question. "That guy wouldn't tell us this stuff if he wasn't going to kill us."

I open my mouth to reassure him, but it turns out that the smarmy man on the PA system can hear us.

"What a clever little boy you are, Charlie," he says in cheery tones, as if he's telling us we've just won a free toaster. "It's very possible that you won't survive the day. But . . . you might. It all depends on your parents."

Charlie's head rears back, hitting my chin on the way. "Don't let them cut off my fingers, Kari!" he begs.

"Well, it's messy, Charlie my boy," the voice muses. "With the blood and bone fragments spraying the glass of the cubes and all . . . not that my men don't have plenty of Windex aboard."

My brother whimpers and hides his head against my chest while my fury grows again. What kind of people terrify small children like this?

I turn my head toward my parents again. Their faces are sheet white, paler even than Gustav's. They're terrified for Charlie. This is exactly the reaction the smarmy guy wants—he's trying to hurt *them* more than my brother.

I feel a burning need to know what this is all about. The USS *Revenge*? Passcodes to the Agency? Explosives set in the building?

"Who are you?" I shout. "What is this about? Why do you hate us so much?"

"I don't hate you, per se, Karina," the voice says. "You're a quid pro quo."

"A what?"

The voice tsks. "Should have studied your Latin."

"Yeah, whatever."

The big main door that we originally came through opens, and a man wearing a headset steps into the passage between the two rows of glass cells.

He's got thinning dark hair combed back into a sparse ponytail; small, ice-blue eyes; and virtually no lips. His skin is a dark olive, and he sports one small diamond stud earring. He's wearing army fatigue pants and an olive T-shirt with combat boots.

I glance at my parents to gauge their reaction.

My mom closes her eyes and bangs her head against their glass wall. My dad drops his head into his hands. Oh, yeah. They know this dude.

"My name is Rafe," he says, as if we're all meeting at a tennis match or something. "Your parents and I used to work together. And they are responsible for the deaths of my own children."

My dad shakes his head.

"Don't you deny it, Cal," Rafe growls. "On that last job, you—and the goddamned Agency—painted a target on their heads and left them unprotected."

Both of my parents speak at once, but of course I can't hear what they're saying. Only Rafe can. But he overrides them.

"Your incompetence, Irine—oh, don't like that word, do you? Your *incompetence* let the target escape. And you, Cal, are worse than incompetent. You placed seeing to your wife's injuries over pursuit and takedown of the target. You prioritized that *bitch* over the job you were sworn to do, the job that I invested five years undercover to set up . . . and it cost me my kids."

My parents are both shaking their heads now.

"Admit it!" Rafe roars. "You *will* acknowledge your guilt. You *will* confess. And you will do it in front of your own children, so that they know exactly who you really are: traitors, selfish screwups, the kind of lowlifes who leave *innocent minors* holding the bag for their crimes."

Huh. I can't say the shoe doesn't fit here.

Are my parents traitors? *Check.*

Selfish? *Check.*

The kind of people who dodge out on kids? *Big, blinking, neon-red check.*

Rafe is breathing heavily now, his anger a palpable thing. "Do you know that the target sent me a home movie, afterward? Of what he did to my Sarah and Ben? Do you have *any idea* what it's like to see something like that? How it plays like a satanic movie reel in my mind every night? Over and over . . . the screaming, the begging, the calls for Daddy to save them . . ." His face contorts and his mouth works. He's unable to go on.

He walks to my dad's cube and slams his fist down on the top. "So now perhaps you all understand why you're here."

Dad stares stonily ahead.

My mom is trembling worse than Charlie—I can see it from three yards away. She's shaking her head and saying no, over and over again.

"Shut up!" Rafe screams at her, running to her cube and kicking the glass.

She freezes, looks him dead in the eyes.

"Say it," he hisses at her. "For once in your life, be honest. Take the blame. *Own it.*"

Mom doesn't open her mouth.

So Rafe turns back to Dad. "You'd better start talking for her." Venom oozes from Rafe's voice. "Or I'll turn Irine over to the ship's crew. They haven't seen a woman in months."

Dad's eyes narrow; a muscle at his jaw jumps, then another. But he says not one word.

"Fine. We'll have some fun with Kari and Charlie first.

Then the crew can have your wife, and you'll watch it all."

Mom starts to shake again.

In another lifetime, maybe I'd feel sorry for her. But not in this one. Charlie and I are probably going to die—painfully and horribly—because of her and my dad. Because of who they are and what they've done.

I ignore the doubts creeping into my head . . . the ones that ask, in all reasonableness, whether it isn't understandable that my dad stopped to save my mom from bad injuries before continuing his mission. The doubts that say the loss of Rafe's kids is the target's fault, not my parents'.

Rafe is half-right and half-wrong. In work for the Agency, a mission trumps everything. Even injuries to a fellow agent, wife or not.

But in all honesty, who could have predicted that the target—whoever it is they're talking about—would go after Rafe's kids?

I don't have much of a chance to philosophize about any of this, though. Because Rafe comes to the door of our cube and looks straight at me.

"I won't enjoy this," he says. "In fact, I won't personally be here to watch. I'm not that kind of man." He swings toward my parents. "But you, Cal and Irine, *will* watch. And in the meantime you'll tell us, in the hopes of saving your daughter's life, where that list of all the KGB2 agents can be found. Oh, yes—I know about that. And I'd find it quite useful."

He smiles serenely and turns back to me. He slides a plastic card into the slot of the keypad next to my cube and gestures to the guards standing nearby. He continues to speak over his shoulder to Mom and Dad.

"However, because you're seasoned agents who've been trained to withstand torture, I expect that Kari will have some broken ribs first. If that doesn't work, we'll break some fingers and toes, or bring the starving rats. You do know what can be done to a girl with rats, don't you?"

Fear rockets from my stomach to my mouth. It has a sour, metallic taste. I have no time to swallow it before the two guards wrench open the door and come for me.

Chapter Twenty

I don't shrink from the guards, as they expect. I lunge at them, my feet and fists flying. I clock one squarely in the temple and he staggers back, then goes down.

The other one has more chops. He blocks my kicks and manages to grab my left wrist. I smash my right elbow into his jaw, knocking his head back, but he won't let go. I smash my elbow into his nose next, and blood sprays over both of us as he curses.

It's in my eyes and I'm distracted, trying to wipe it with my sleeve, when Rafe gets me with a stun gun. It drops me in electrified agony, and I black out.

When I awake, cold water's being thrown in my face and I know I'm totally screwed. I'm hanging by my bound wrists from a hook in a larger cell by myself. No, Charlie's huddled in the corner, his hands tied at the wrists. My parents are opposite, in separate cells.

The tops of my big toes just barely brush the floor. Though my hands and wrists have gone numb, all the blood has rushed from my arms, and my shoulders scream in agony.

A guard in a black ski mask throws another cup of freezing water into my face. I choke and sputter. His eyes are small, black, and devoid of expression. He appears bored, as if he does stuff like this on a routine basis. I find that terrifying.

Rafe's voice comes over the speaker system. He's no longer in the passageway.

"So, Calvin. We'll start with you. How much do you think the Agency would pay for that list of the KGB2 agents?"

"I have no idea," my dad says.

"Wrong answer." Rafe sighs. "Virgil, you may begin. For every wrong answer, you know what to do."

The guard to my right flexes his hand. Then before I can brace myself, he punches me hard in the stomach.

The impact—and the pain—knocks the breath out of me.

Given my position, I can't double over, so I writhe, drawing my knees upward, and fight for air. My one consolation is that I didn't shriek.

Charlie, poor Charlie. He almost passes out, I think. Then he crabwalks backward from where he was sitting. He backs into the far corner of the cell, hugs himself, and rocks back and forth. His eyes are the size of dinner plates.

"You coward," my dad spits. "Beating up on a girl half your size."

There's no shame in the guard's eyes. If anything, he looks even more bored.

"Cal," Rafe says again. "How much?"

"Hell, I don't—a few million, at least!"

"Better answer. Now, who could authorize, say, a ten-million-dollar wire transfer to my account?"

"It would have to be authorized and countersigned by at least two high-level managers," my dad says quickly.

"Wrong answer."

The guard to my left punches me in the ribs.

I do gasp with the pain this time; I can't help it. His fist feels like a sledgehammer.

"I didn't ask the procedure, Cal. I asked for specific names. Now, would it be Dave Winslow? Sheila O'Toole? Or perhaps Alan Chung?

"Alan and Sheila," Dad says quickly.

"Excellent. Now, where exactly can I find the list, Calvin?"

My dad's voice is weak as he says, "I don't know."

My mom winces and sucks in a breath.

Rafe sighs. "Wrong answer."

The next blow cracks one of my ribs. I hear it, as if from far away, but I feel it in excruciating detail. I still don't shriek, but I do pant like a dog from the pain, and sweat rolls from my temples down my cheeks and to my neck.

Funny, but the physical pain I feel isn't as bad as the emotional pain all over again that my dad is betraying me. I think he knows exactly where that list is.

"Where is it, Cal?" Rafe's voice has become a singsong.

"I don't know! Please don't hit her!" There is a certain amount of anguish in his voice—I'll give him that. But not enough to give up the location of his precious list.

This blow slams into my kidneys. Bile shoots up my throat and out of my mouth. I have no control over it, since I'm keening like an animal. There's truly no dignity in the face of this level of pain.

I swing back and forth from the force of the blow.

The sick twist of a guard flexes his fingers, then eyes me as if I'm a sack of flour.

Stuff dribbles out of my mouth and down my chin and neck. When I can catch half a breath, I croak, "Rot. In. Hell."

The guard sneers, thinking I mean him.

Then I add, "Dad." I tap into my crazy anger at my parents so that I have something to focus on other than agony.

My dad's face registers shock, then goes utterly blank. Then he shouts, "I take responsibility, Rafe! I'm sorry. So sorry. For what happened to Sarah and Ben."

A long hiss comes over the speaker system. "Well, isn't that special, Cal."

"I screwed up," my dad admits. "I shouldn't have let myself get . . . sidetracked."

My mom's head rears back. She gazes at him with an emotion I have trouble reading. Shock? No. A sense of betrayal? No. Oh, my God—it's *contempt*.

Rafe takes a deep breath. "That must be music to Irine's ears. Thank you, Cal. Unfortunately, at this point, it's too damn little and too damn late. You had your chance before, and you didn't take it."

Dad groans.

"Where's the list, Irine?" Rafe sings.

"Let me take Kari's place!" my mom shouts. "Please, for the love of God!"

"Wrooooong answer . . ."

The guard breaks another of my ribs. I can't help it this time; I scream.

Charlie rockets out of his corner and jumps on the man, screeching and howling. "Stop it! Stop it!" He beats on him with his powerless, seven-year-old fists.

The guard easily grabs him by the collar and holds him a foot off the ground, Charlie's legs and arms still swinging like windmills. "Don't you hit my sister!" he yells.

The guard shakes him until his teeth rattle and tosses him against a wall of the cube. Charlie's head smacks against it, and he slides down, dazed and cowed.

My mom lets out a sound somewhere between a moan and a whimper.

"Take me instead," Dad begs. "Don't do this to my daughter."

"Oooh, Cal. *Really* wrong answer. Would you like to see—"

The guard punches me in the kidneys again, and I vomit on him, to my satisfaction but also my shame.

He reacts with disgust, like an actual human being might, wiping the stuff off his shirt.

I just hang there, panting.

Rafe continues on the speaker. "Would you like to see the videotape of what the target did to my Sarah? I think you should. Then you'll think twice about asking me for mercy." He pauses. "That's enough on the body, Anton. Take her down. Let's start breaking fingers."

I can't say I like the sound of this much. But I try to focus on the relief I will feel in my arms and shoulders. That's something, isn't it? I'm desperate for anything positive to hang on to. I may hate my mom right now, but an old piece of her advice pops into my head: *When you're in a bad place, darling, take yourself mentally somewhere else.*

The truth is that even Tech 101 class sounds wonderful right now, compared to this. I try to take myself there, because I can't think of anything else.

As Anton pulls me off the hook and dumps me into a chair, I focus also on the fact that I'd rather have broken fingers than *no* fingers. And if it comes right down to it, I'd rather have no fingers than rats inside me. I shudder uncontrollably at the thought.

Anton ties one of my legs to a chair leg. When he goes for the other, I kick him, just for the hell of it, even though I have little energy left.

He backhands me across the face. Awesome—a clear sign that our relationship is lightening up. Anton unties my wrists, squinting at me to see if I'll hit him. But both of my arms are buzzing like hives of hornets, and I have absolutely no strength in them. So I fantasize about blackening both his eyes instead, because that's easier than bearing the pain of trying to sit up with broken ribs and pulverized kidneys.

"Comfortable, Kari?" Rafe asks politely over the speaker.

I roll my eyes up toward it and force myself to grin. I have no energy to think up a snappy comeback.

"Now, where were we?" he asks. "Oh, yes. Where's the KGB2 list?"

Neither of my parents says a word.

Anton grabs my right index finger.

"Tell them, you assholes!" I shriek. "I know you have it! You stole it from the Agency and took it to Russia!"

"Wrong. Answer." Rafe's voice is arctic.

Anton bends my finger backward until it snaps in a vicious symphony of pain.

I've never even *heard* a sound like the one that comes from deep down inside me.

Then I black out.

Here we go with the ice water in the face again. Passing out has become old hat for me at this point—almost routine. I try to count the number of times it's happened in the last couple of weeks, distracting myself as Rafe asks the same question again.

Let's see . . . Evan choked me out at GI. Evan jabbed a needle into my arm in . . . where was that? Paris as well? Or Munich? Murnau? It's a blur. Now it's happened here in the belly of the freakin' USS *Revenge*—what a lame joke, by the way—three times. Wait—is that right? I look down and check my fingers.

Four times, judging by the fact that every finger on my right hand is broken.

The pain is a dull roar at this point, but it localizes and screams with each new break. Still, I'm so exhausted by it that I can't even summon the energy to flinch as Rafe asks the question again. "This is becoming very boring, people," he adds.

As Anton grasps my thumb, a commotion breaks out above us. Heavily booted feet, running. Shots being fired? I'm not sure. Shouting. Banging. More possible gunfire. More shouting.

Fortunately for me, the noise distracts both Rafe and Anton.

I see hope dawning on Charlie's face as he gazes toward the door. Hope that maybe we're being rescued.

I'm not sure I can spell "h-o-p-e" at this point, but I inwardly cheer on my brother's.

Why won't Rafe do us the courtesy of giving a blow-by-blow "sportscast" of what's going on over the speakers, since he loves giving commentary so much? Go figure.

It's a few minutes before we hear clanging right above us—it's coming from the narrow metal stairs. Several sets of boots.

Charlie jumps up.

My parents exchange glances.

I just hunch over in my stew of pain, barely caring.

The big door flies open, and two figures are marched in by more armed guards, hands bound behind their backs: Evan and Kale.

I'm perversely both thrilled and horrified to see them. Thrilled because it means they tried to come and rescue me and Charlie. Horrified because they're now going to die with us.

They both spot me at the same time. Kale's jaw goes

slack with shock. I guess I don't look too pretty at this point.

While they shove Kale into a cell, Evan goes nuts. "What have you done to her?!" He lunges at one guard, head-butting him, and tries to kick out at another, but they've learned their lesson and they've got his feet bound so that he only has about a foot of cord between them in order to walk.

Still, he jumps into the air and slams both feet into the stomach of another guard, who falls to the floor clutching himself. Evan crashes to the floor himself.

The first guard bashes him over the head with a heavy flashlight.

"You arseholes!" Evan shouts. He spots my parents. "And you—why the hell are you here? You should be lined up in front of a bloody firing squad!"

I couldn't agree more.

"Kari—are you okay?" he asks, still choking on rage. He can clearly see that I'm not.

I still have the barest atom of energy for sarcasm. "Dude," I manage. "Been a party down here. Balloons. Cake. Show tunes."

"Christ . . ." His face is drawn, his lips flat. His eyes snap with fury. There's a bruise on his cheekbone and his shirt is torn. The guards drag him to a cell.

Before they shut the door on him, I produce a smile. "Evan. Thanks for trying. Can't believe you messed up your hair for me . . ."

Chapter Twenty-One

I can't imagine that things can get worse, but they do, after a brief respite. Rafe forgets the speakers are on as he demands an accounting of what happened, so we get the full story. Evan and Kale approached this ship on a smaller boat that they probably stole. They boarded using climbing equipment, and between them they took down six of Rafe's men before they were simply outnumbered and outgunned. It was truly a heroic attempt, and I'm just thankful they weren't shot.

"How in the hell did they track us here?" Rafe demands.

"We're not sure, sir," says the man briefing him. "Somehow they must have followed us."

Rafe swears.

He can swear all he wants as long as they don't discover our GPS chips. Even if we're dead by the time anyone else locates us, I want Rafe and his buddies to pay.

I wonder where Matthis and Rita are at this point. I hope they're safe.

"You can go," Rafe tells the man. And his attention returns to extracting the information he wants.

My good buddy Anton returns and flexes his fingers in front of our cell.

My mouth goes dry, my mind blanks, and my nerves scream. Not again. I don't think I can take anymore. I really don't.

Rafe says, "Since we haven't gotten results with her, let's start with the little twerp."

"*No!*" My parents and I scream it simultaneously.

Charlie shrinks back into his corner, eyes huge. He shoves his hands under his bottom, and my heart breaks in that moment.

Anton opens the door of the cell and steps in.

My feet are tied to the chair, my whole body is in agony, and my right hand is useless. I lunge for him anyway, dragging the chair behind me. Of course I fall, the chair careening down on top of me, and Anton laughs.

I push backward desperately with my one good hand, trying to move my body between him and Charlie.

Anton simply steps around me, and when I grab at his legs, he kicks me off and stomps on my left hand.

"You're not getting him!" I shriek.

But he does.

Charlie fights silently. He doesn't make it easy. But in the end, he's only seven years old, and his forty-two-pound body is no match for Anton's two-hundred-pound one.

I sob on the floor as Anton ties him to a chair.

My mom is pounding her forehead against the glass of her cell, screaming to Rafe to take her instead.

My dad has scooted to the far corner of his and turned his back. His shoulders shake.

Everyone else in captivity just looks horrified.

"Tell him, you jerks!" I yell again. "Tell him where the list is! What is *wrong* with you? How can you let this—"

I'm interrupted by gunshots. There's no mistaking it this time—these are high-powered automatic weapons being fired.

"Lock all the cell doors!" orders Rafe to Anton. "Then stand guard just inside the main door. Await further orders."

I have no idea what's going on, but I'm so relieved that Charlie's not being hurt that I'm not sure I care. More shots sound just above us as I try to crawl to my brother. Gunfire erupts just outside the door as the pain threatens to overwhelm me in a blanket of trauma, but I refuse to pass out again.

Militants dressed in black stream down the stairs and rappel from railings everywhere. Rafe and Anton the guard vanish into the chaos.

Someone lets us out of our cell, and my parents as well. They rush to me. "W-why?" I croak. Bile and screaming do wonders for the throat. I sound like a three-pack-a-day smoker. "Why didn't you t-tell them? Where the list is? Why?"

My mom's face falls and my dad shuts his eyes tightly.

It makes me angry, fuels my sense of betrayal. "Look at me!"

He does. Then two of the military guys in black pull my parents away, and it seems to me that they don't protest too much.

Another man, a guy who looks familiar, crouches next to me with a medical bag. He *tsks* and eases up my shirt, which scrapes and burns. I'm struggling to place him in my memory when he puts a hand on my ribs. Even though his touch is gentle, it's agony.

While I'm focusing on just dealing with the pain, he injects me with something, and frankly I welcome it. I'm enveloped soon by a warm, fuzzy, floating sensation. I think maybe he shot me full of Demerol. Whatever it is, I'm intensely grateful for it as the guy—*where* have I seen him before?—bandages my ribs, then starts on my fingers. I can feel a dull throbbing in my left hand, the one Anton stepped on. But I can't feel the right one at all because this medic has also given me a local anesthetic.

I turn my head toward Charlie, who's holding my aching left hand. "Hey, Charlie Brown," I croak. A shadow hovers over us. I crane my neck and roll my eyes upward to find that it's my dad. He's crouched right by my head.

"I'm so sorry, baby," he says, smoothing my hair.

Maybe it's the cloud of Demerol, but I can't summon the willpower to hate him right now. "You came . . . to get us."

He nods. There are tears in his eyes. "We love you. We love you and Charlie very much."

"Then why . . . *why*, Dad?" I fight to push the happy cloud away. I want answers. "You owe us an explanation— at the very least."

Just as he opens his mouth, gunshots explode above us again. I hear more heavy, booted feet pounding. And shouts.

"Interpol!" a voice thunders. "We have you surrounded! Drop your weapons!"

The guy bandaging me freaks out. He jumps up and glares at my dad, then spits something in Russian. And that's when I figure it out. He looks familiar because this is the same guy who tried to kidnap me, with that woman, off the train. What the—?

My dad answers him, in rapid-fire Russian.

My brother understands it, but I don't. "Charlie, what are they saying?"

The man gestures to us, shaking his head, and makes a chopping motion with his hand.

It's not hard to interpret in any language, and Charlie gasps, clenching my hand. His own trembles.

My dad shouts something at the man, then tackles him. They both go flying, and Charlie winces as they start whaling on each other. My dad is the bigger and stronger of the two, though, and he quickly gains the advantage, knocking the Russian unconscious.

Dad wipes his face on his sleeve and comes back to us. "Kari. Charlie. Your mother and I have to go."

Charlie sucks in a breath, then wraps his arms around his knees and rocks back and forth.

I stare up at Dad. "But—"

"You'll be safe, all right?"

"No, not all right!" My tongue feels thick. "You tell me what's going on—"

Dad looks at me for a second, then grabs the semiconscious

Russian by the belt and the collar, and muscles him out the door and up the stairs.

I'm so confused. And I'm getting angry again, despite the false sense of well-being that the Demerol provides. "Charlie, what was that all about?"

"That guy wanted to kill us. Before he and Dad left."

This makes absolutely no sense. "Then why did the guys in black come to rescue us? Why was the Russian man bandaging me and giving me painkillers?"

"Um," says Charlie. "I think it has to do with . . . well, if we were going with them, then it was fine. But if we weren't, because they had to leave fast and you're injured, then it wasn't okay."

The old philosophy of "kill the wounded so they don't slow you down." Nice. I'm still nowhere close to understanding, but I have a very bad feeling that the Russian and his buddies in black are KGB2 guys. "Okay, Charlie. I guess we'll figure it all out eventually. In the meantime, I think that guy lying dead in the doorway is my buddy Anton the guard, and he's got one of the key cards in his pocket. So why don't you let our friends out of those cells?"

He nods and gets to his feet. He walks over to Anton and crouches down next to him, looking a little freaked out at having to touch a dead body.

"Just don't think about it too hard, kiddo," I say. "And he wasn't exactly a nice guy."

Charlie closes his eyes and digs into Anton's pocket. He pulls out the key card and backs away quickly, almost sprinting to Evan's cell.

"Thank you, little man," Evan says as he steps out. He ruffles Charlie's hair.

Then he rushes over to me and kisses me right on the mouth. I feel it all the way to my toes—unless that's still the Demerol. I'm really glad that somebody wiped the blood, vomit, and bile off my face, but even so, I can't possibly look or smell very good right now.

"Dear God, Kari," he murmurs, pulling back and evaluating me. "You're the bravest girl I know." He takes my good hand and looks up at the ceiling for a long moment, his mouth working. I'm initially puzzled at the odd expression on his face, and then I realize that Evan—*Evan*, of all people—is struggling to hold back tears. For me.

I'm still surfing the wave of Demerol—which is doing its best to knock me out—so I can't really take this in, and I don't know what to do with the involuntary clench of my stomach in response. But it vaguely hurts. I can't be clenching anything right now, not even my teeth.

"Crybaby," I say provocatively.

His mouth works some more as he meets my gaze almost tenderly. "Shrew."

I struggle to sit up, since we need to find out what's going on. Boy, is that a bad idea, even on painkillers.

"Cut it out," Evan orders. Then he gently slips his big hands under my arms and eases me up. He seems to know by instinct that sitting is too painful, so he pulls me straight to my feet. I wobble on them, then establish a better balance. "Okay?" he asks.

"Yep. Thanks."

Evan looks as if he might kiss me again, but then his mouth flattens and he looks away.

Good thing, because there's a clatter of more boots on the stairs and then a bunch of uniforms burst in, weapons at the ready. Rebecca Morrow is at their head, in full combat gear and with her long, black curly hair stuffed up into a helmet. "Interpol! Hands up!"

She casts a quick, evaluative glance at me, and I see shock roll over her face. "Oh, Kari," she murmurs, her mouth softening. "Honey, I'm so sorry." But she's got a job to do, a team to run. She's not going to take me in her arms and rock me to sleep—and I can't expect her to. Within seconds, she's distracted and barking out orders.

Charlie, meanwhile, has let out Kale and is headed toward the Duvernays.

"Hands up!" someone else roars, and my brother freezes in his tracks.

The four of us, along with everyone else, put our hands in the air—Kale and Evan help me with mine—until we're told to relax. The Interpol team acknowledges that we're GI, searches for anyone in hiding, lets out Gustav and his grandfather, and secures the rest of the ship.

"Where are Matthis and Rita?" I ask Kale.

"Rita was pissed, but we made them change hotels and stay in Salzburg in case something went wrong," he says. "Neither of them has any combat training whatsoever." He looks me up and down. "Jesus, Kari. We need to get you to a hospital. They can meet us there."

I nod, since I can't really argue with my need for

medical attention. I could have internal injuries, for all I know.

Evan and Kale help load me onto a stretcher that the Interpol people bring down.

As my eyes roll backward, I say, "Ha. Should be fun getting me up those stairs, guys. Sucks to be you."

And then the fog closes in once again.

Chapter Twenty-Two

Big surprise that I wake up in the hospital with an IV stuck into my left hand. I feel like one big giant bruise. My entire torso appears to be bandaged and taped, and my right hand is a bouquet of splints. No karate for a while.

Charlie's asleep at the very foot of my bed, curled into a little ball. Someone's wrapped a blanket around him. Evan and Matthis are in chairs next to me. Kale and Rita are sprawled on the floor, sitting against the wall, another blanket wrapped around their shoulders.

"Look who's back among the living," Evan says softly. He leans forward and takes my hand, careful not to dislodge the IV drip.

"Hi." My voice comes out in a rasp.

"Hey," Matthis says. "Welcome back."

"Water?" Rita offers me a cup with a goose-necked straw that bends down to my parched lips.

"Thanks." I suck down about half the cup at once.

"Easy," Kale cautions me. "Your stomach's taken a beating."

Sure enough, some of the water tries to come back up, and I struggle to keep it down.

I notice that they're all looking at me as if I just escaped from the zoo. "What?"

"Nothing," Rita says too quickly.

I squint at her. I put a hand up to my face and discover that a lot of it is puffy. Well, go figure. My good friend Anton had smacked me on one side of it, and then when I fell forward in the chair trying to protect Charlie, the other side had smashed into the floor. "Let me guess: I won't be winning the Miss Teen USA contest today?"

Evan's lips twitch. "Maybe tomorrow," he says diplomatically.

Since I can't change my face, I change the subject. "So what happened on the ship?"

"Hang on," Evan says. "Let me get Rebecca and Stefan and Abby." He gets up and goes to the door.

That's when I hear Abby's raised voice coming from the hallway, where she's arguing with her parents. "There's *no* reason why I shouldn't go skiing with Cecily! She has a chalet at Klosters. That's, like, one of the coolest ski resorts anywhere. And I can stay for *free!*"

"There *is* a reason," Rebecca says. "We don't think it's a healthy friendship. And she's not a good influence on you."

"So now you get to choose my friends for me?" Abby shouts.

"Lower your voice, Abigail, and don't take that tone with your mother," her dad, Stefan, tells her.

Evan sticks his head out. "Guys, Kari's awake."

"Wonderful!" exclaims Rebecca. She bustles in. Her wild black curly hair is clipped on top of her head, and she's wearing a deep amethyst turtleneck with black trousers. She's curvy enough to seem like your average mom in regular clothes, but in shorts and a tank she looks like an Olympic athlete. The woman is *cut.* She smells of jasmine and Ivory soap as she bends forward to kiss my puffy cheek. "How are you feeling, honey?"

"Truth? Like I've been fed through a wood chipper and glued back together."

"Oh, dear." Stefan comes to stand by her. He's been on sabbatical working on a book, so I'm surprised to see him here. He's grown a beard lately, probably because he sometimes forgets to shave while he's researching a project. He's such the absentminded professor, cliché or not.

I'd never put him with Rebecca in a hundred years, but he was once her "asset," to use a spy term, and maybe the top agent at Interpol wants to be able to just relax and laugh with someone nonthreatening when she's at home.

Stefan peers down at me through smudged reading glasses. His brown eyes are kindly but abstracted, as if he's translating a text in another corner of his head—and as a linguistics specialist, he probably is. There's a cracker crumb caught in his beard.

Rebecca notices the cracker crumb and frowns. I can tell she wants to brush it out but doesn't want to embarrass him.

So Abby does it for her. She pushes around them, rolls her eyes, flicks the crumb out of her dad's beard, and says, "Wow, Kari. We were scared that you'd go into a coma. You okay?"

"I'm awesome," I say, staring at all the splints on my hand. "I'll be putting on nail polish in no time."

I look at Rebecca. "We were never so glad to see someone as you. But how did you know to come?"

Her mouth tightens as she looks at her daughter. "Abby called me while I was in the field, said it was an emergency—"

"I told her I was pregnant!" Abby says with a mischievous twinkle in her eyes. "Go figure—she got on the next flight home."

Stefan's lips twitch. "Knocking back Jack the whole way."

Rebecca smacks him. "Too much information!"

"I beg your pardon, my dear," Stefan says drily. "Of course you were sipping tea—with quiet maternal joy—and knitting yellow booties with ducks on them."

"Freaks," Abby mutters. "My parents are freaks."

"So what happened on the ship?" I ask again. "After I passed out?"

"Do you want the good news or the bad news first?" Rita asks.

"Good news."

"Okay. All the terrorists are either dead or detained in custody."

"And the bad news?"

"Most of the KGB2 operatives got away, except for two. But they can't be interrogated because they're dead.

Worse, the *jungbrunnen* is missing, as well as the list of Agency passcodes. They must have taken both."

My mouth twists. I think of the other list, the notorious list of KGB2 people that Mom and Dad have "no" knowledge of. Right. "My parents?"

"Escaped. The Duvernays as well."

While I'm sort of glad that Gustav and his grandfather got out of Dodge, I really don't know how to feel about Mom and Dad getting away. They would have been imprisoned and interrogated . . . possibly tortured, depending on what facility in which country they were taken to. Let's just say that the Geneva Convention doesn't always apply in these situations, and I have no illusions about that.

I wouldn't wish torture on anyone, having been through it. And I don't want my parents to suffer. I may not like it, but I do still love them. They're my parents and they raised me. To their credit, they did attempt a rescue of Charlie and me. I can't forget that.

But what damage will they cause to the US and Europe? The Agency? A dull pain throbs inside me that has nothing to do with my injuries. How can I both love and despise these people? I close my eyes.

It makes no sense to me that they are working with KGB2, none at all. Unless there's something in my mom's past that I don't know about, something that would force her into it, and my dad with her?

I turn that over in my mind. This theory has a lot more appeal than them just doing it for money. They're not like that. And they came to rescue me and Charlie. And my dad kicked the Russian doc's ass when he wanted to kill us . . . they're being blackmailed into working with KGB2. I'm sure of it. And with that certainty comes a measure of relief. I'm still angry and I still have questions, but I feel a little less betrayed.

I talk with everyone some more, trying to absorb energy from Rita's obnoxious fringed orange sweater, but fatigue steamrollers me and my eyelids keep drooping closed. Like a narcoleptic, I fall asleep in the middle of the conversation.

When I open my eyes, Luke Carson is standing in front of me, juggling a vase of flowers, a bunch of balloons, a box of chocolates, *and* a teddy bear.

Evan drops my hand as if it burned him.

Luke registers that and frowns, tightening his grip on the teddy bear's leg. It's dangling upside down.

I blink, because I'm sure I'm hallucinating.

But he's still there, still smiling a guilty, hopeful, apologetic smile. "Kari?"

"*Luke?* What are you doing here?" I keep waiting to feel something. Excitement or chills or butterflies. But I feel … nothing. Nothing but a vague surprise that he's in front of me. Maybe I've had too much trauma and too many drugs.

Evan stands up, looking as if someone died. He gives a nod to Luke and heads for the door. Everyone else takes this as a cue too. They all troop out.

Luke shifts from one foot to the other, and then back. He's so hot . . . he hasn't changed a bit.

I take in his athletic, Abercrombie & Fitch good looks: the brush-cut blond hair, the chocolate-brown eyes, the tanned face even in winter, from constantly running track outside. Again, I wait to feel that rush I used to feel whenever he looked in my direction.

But I don't.

All I feel is a muted kind of sadness.

What's wrong with me?

"Kari," he says. "How are you?"

"Okay, I guess." I aim a weak smile at him.

He scans me and then averts his gaze. Wow, I guess I look really bad. But I can't bring myself to care.

"Look. I just want to apologize—" He breaks off into an awkward silence. Still loaded down with that overkill of silly stuff that I don't even want, he cracks his neck. He looks supremely uncomfortable.

In one of those weird, instantaneous moments of clarity, I get it. There's nothing wrong with me. This thing with Luke is just not right. Even though I desperately want it to be.

I shake my head. "No need to apologize."

"Yeah," he says heavily. "There is." He makes no move to put down any of the stuff in his arms. "I shouldn't have taken Tessa to that formal. I shouldn't have even thought about it."

Tessa. Wouldn't it be easy to blame her? The "other woman"?

"So, how was it?" I ask, even though I'm not sure I want to know the answer. "The dance, I mean."

A flush spreads up his neck. "Oh. Fine, I guess."

So he went, even though he knew it would upset me. "What did she wear?"

"Uh, blue." Luke stares intently at the balloons, as if he's an archaeologist and they are ancient skulls that will reveal the secrets to some long-lost civilization. He won't meet my gaze.

"Did you have fun?"

"Kari . . ."

I know, deep down, that they fooled around that night. I just know. And even though I tell myself that he was free, that we were technically broken up, it still hurts.

"It's fine, Luke. It's done. We weren't together, anyway."

"I'm sorry," he mumbles again.

There's a long, awkward moment. I need to put us both out of this misery.

I open my mouth, then close it again. What am I, stupid? I've already broken up with Luke once. No girl in her right mind would break up with him *twice*.

No girl except me.

"Luke," I finally manage. "This . . . relationship, or whatever it is. It's not working. We both know it. The distance, the fact that we don't know each other all that well . . ." I shake my head again. "The Tessa factor . . ."

"There's no Tessa factor," he says quickly. "I swear. One-time thing."

Poor Tessa.

"And the distance—look, Kari, I'm here now. I flew all this way to see you. To make things right. So the distance isn't a factor."

But it is. I shake my head slowly. "Luke. You're visiting

for, what? Two or three days? A week? But then you'll go back to DC, and I'll go back to Paris. You'll speak English and I'll speak French." *Perish the thought.* "You'll be training for the track team and I'll be . . ."

I'll be training for an Interpol mission, or tracking down a terrorist, or who knows what.

"Our lives are too different, Luke," I say.

He stares at me, incredulous. "I just traveled *twelve hours* to see you, and you're breaking up with me? *Again?*"

No, I want to tell him. *You're right. I'm nuts. I'm ungrateful.*

But something—is it pride? Common sense? Deep, totally inconvenient inner knowledge?—won't let me.

I nod.

Luke looks down at his feet. He looks at the wall. He looks out the window. In short, he looks anywhere but at me.

He doesn't protest anymore. But he does look pissed.

Then his face goes carefully, deliberately neutral. It's the look of a guy who is too cool to acknowledge hurt.

He tucks the teddy bear next to Charlie, who's oblivious, still sleeping through all this. He sets the vase down on a table along with the chocolates. And then he approaches the bed and ties the balloons to the foot of it, all without saying a word.

He stares at me for a long moment. Then he sighs. Gives one short nod.

Luke reaches forward and gives my toe, under the blankets, an affectionate squeeze. "Kari, what can I say? You're an amazing girl. You're so brave. You know the truth: that we're not right for each other. And you're not afraid to say it, the way most people are." He swallows. "The way I am."

Wow. That's quite an admission. I look at him with new respect.

"Yeah. Well." Not that I know what the appropriate response is here.

"I need to tell you something before I leave." He hesitates, clearly struggling with what he wants—or doesn't want—to say. "As long as we're saying stuff that's crappy, and awkward, and . . . and unwelcome? Well, there's a guy outside in the hallway who *is* right for you. Evan. The guy who paid for a transatlantic flight from DC to Vienna and told me I'd better be on it, or he'd personally fly across the pond, kick my ass, and drag me back with him."

I gape at Luke. "He did *not*."

"Oh, yeah, Kari." Luke smiles wryly at me. "He did." He walks to the door. "And, by the way, he's also the one who paid for Rita and Kale's flights. Want me to send him in?"

My mouth is still hanging open. I finally shut it. *Evan* bought Luke's ticket? And the others? Why?

Then I nod.

"Okay. Listen, Kari . . ." He sighs. His eyes full of regret, he lifts a hand and waves. "I'll see you around."

I muster up a weak grin. "Well, probably not. It's kind of a long swim."

Chapter Twenty-Three

"What—why—why is Luke leaving?" Evan asks, clearly at a loss when he comes back in.

"Because we broke up," I tell him.

His face falls, which is the very last thing I'd expect, given the way he's been acting around me lately. Kissing me. Holding my hand. Looking as if he was on the way to a funeral when Luke walked in. He raises his hands into the air, then drops them again. "But—"

I stare at him.

Evan Kincaid, International Jerk of Mystery, is visibly flustered. He actually runs a hand through his hair, sending the careful styling into weird tufts.

"You're messing up your do again," I point out. "Why?"

He cocks his head to one side and evaluates me. "I . . . uh. Well, it's just that . . ."

"What, Evan? Spit it out."

"If you two have broken up, then I don't bloody well have a Christmas gift for you, then, do I? And this was perfect. You've bollocksed it up, right and proper."

I take a moment to absorb this and then start laughing. Laughing is pain. Lots of pain—ribs, stomach, kidneys, everywhere. But I can't help it.

"What's so bloody funny, then, you daft cow?" But he, too, breaks into a grin.

"C-cow?" I gasp.

He raises an eyebrow. "It's a term of endearment. A British thing. You wouldn't understand, Yank."

I catch my breath. "Evan, why would you want to, um, use a 'term of endearment' with me? Just curious."

His mouth twists. He fidgets. He actually runs a hand over the back of his neck and stares out the window. Color blooms in two spots high on his cheekbones. "Because I'm fond of you."

Fond? Who uses words like that?

Evan Kincaid, apparently.

"Could you, um, maybe use a term from the twenty-first century?" I ask him softly. "A lowly . . . I don't know . . . *Yank* term, maybe?"

He puts his hands on his hips, clearly exasperated and uncomfortable.

I peer up at him from under my lashes and try really hard not to smile.

"Right, then."

Evan's eyes have gone from smoky gray to dark blue. The way his eyes change fascinates me. I used to not trust him because of it, but now I think it's cool.

"So." I smooth the blankets next to me.

"So." He takes a step forward, looking down. "A twenty-first century, Yankish word is what you want? You're not demanding at all, are you?"

"Nope." I wait.

He says exactly nothing.

I've never seen Evan Kincaid this way. He flushes bright pink. He opens and closes his mouth like a guppy.

And it's at this moment when I realize something that maybe I should have figured out long before now: I really, really like Evan. Yes, *that* way. I can't help it.

He's annoying, but he's also awesome.

He's totally untrustworthy, but he's always got my back.

He's my tormentor, but he's also my hero.

He's unbelievably hot, but he's got this unexpected, sweet, dorky side buried under all that muscle, all that snooty tailoring. . . .

I'm trying not to laugh again when he shouts, "What the bloody hell is wrong with *'fond,'* anyway?"

"Nothing, Evan," I say in soothing tones. "I'm, uh, *fond* of you, too."

"Don't you dare make fun of me!" he thunders, his face deepening to scarlet.

"Wouldn't dream of it." I bite my lip, hard. I really want the idiot to kiss me, but I'm not sure how to go about it, given his current mood. What would Lacey Carson do?

What would—*ugh*—Cecily Alarie do? The answer is simple: get devious.

"Evan, could you come here to help me with something? Just for a minute?"

He eyes me suspiciously. "Fine," he mutters gracelessly. He walks over to my hospital bed.

I reach my hand out toward him.

He takes it, almost reluctantly.

I pull him down toward me. "I'm having boy trouble."

He squints. "*What* bloody boy? Christ, did I pay thousands of dollars to fly the wrong bloke over here, then?"

I shake my head. "Well, yes," I amend. "The right one's already here in Austria."

He looks puzzled for a moment. Then disgusted. "*Gustav*," he groans. "No, really, Kari. I forbid it! *Anyone* but him—"

"You *forbid* it? Listen, Evan, who do you think you are, the king of England? You can't dictate which guy I have trouble with! It's *so* none of your business—" I break off, perplexed. "Well, I guess it sort of *is*."

He stares at me like I'm the crazy person that I am.

How did this get so screwed up?

"Shut *up*, Evan," I say.

"I wasn't talking!"

"Never mind that. *There is this guy*," I say loudly. "And I *really* want to kiss him right now, but I've had the stuffing beat out of me and I can't reach him. Anything you might be able to do about that?"

"Oh," says Evan. There's a long pause. He looks a bit dazed.

Duh. Superspies? Sometimes they're not so bright.

I wait while he stands there like an ox. "Evan?"

"Well . . . well, but . . . why didn't you say so?"

"I've been trying!"

Evan sits down on the bed next to me, still holding my hand. He keeps staring at me.

I start to wonder—I really do—if with my pulverized face and torn hair, I look so ugly that he can't bring himself to even pity-kiss such a train wreck.

Finally he leans forward, an expression of tenderness on his face, and covers my mouth with his. This weird electric shock runs through my whole body. This time, I know it's not the Demerol.

It's all Evan Kincaid.

I'm not even sure how much time has gone by when somebody bustles in the door. Somebody wearing high heels that clatter on the tile and a big cloud of French perfume. Somebody who comes to a shocked halt and makes a weird hiccup of outrage.

Evan lifts his head, and we both look into the pissed-off face of Cecily Alarie.

"I 'eard you were injured," she says stiffly. "I come to zee 'ow you are, Kari." *Kah-rrhee.*

"*Oh, très bien, vraiment bien, merci!*" I say, enjoying French for the very first time. "That's so, um, nice of you, Cecily. But you look a little, oh, I don't know—*green.* You feeling okay yourself? Did you not sleep well?"

"I am peerfectly fine," she says with a huff. "And 'ow are you, Ehvahn?"

We all know that the true purpose of her visit is to see him. I'm just a convenient excuse. She's so transparent.

"I'm peachy, Cecily. Thank you for asking. But if you could just give me a couple more minutes with my girlfriend? Then I'll be right out. I've got some questions for you."

Oh. My. God.

Evan Kincaid just called me his girlfriend.

Cecily blinks once, then twice. Then looks at me, with my swollen puffy face and torn hair and totally unglamorous hospital gown, in disbelief. Her lips tremble slightly. And then she turns on her high heels and marches out the door, forgetting to set down the vase of flowers she brought.

I cannot look at Evan, because if I do, he will see the unholy glee in my eyes. He will be able to tell that I am not a nice person, not at all.

"Kari?" he says softly.

"Huh?" I focus on smoothing the annoying crease in the sheet under my blanket and marvel that Charlie keeps sleeping through everything.

He reaches out an index finger, puts it under my chin, and forces it upward. "Look at me."

My eyes fly up to meet his. I know I'm smirking, but I can't help it.

"Shrew," he says, smirking right back at me. He doesn't think less of me at all.

We're back in Paris, spending the rest of the holiday with the Morrows. The city lights are twinkling under a fresh blanket of white snow, and the whole house smells of pine and Christmas cookies hot out of the oven. Rita and Matthis have been baking.

Rebecca has put on traditional holiday music, even though as the daughter of Turkish diplomats, she wasn't raised Christian. Stefan stands off to the side pretending to conduct the orchestra as "O, Tannenbaum" plays.

Abby is clearly embarrassed by her dad's goofiness, but I think he's funny, with his curly hair topped by a Santa hat and cookie crumbs caught in what's now been trimmed down to his goatee.

Kale, Charlie, and I are building a very tall gingerbread house. Evan claims to be supervising, but in reality he's watching a movie.

Truth to tell, the gingerbread "house" is becoming a cathedral.

"We're going to have to add flying buttresses," Charlie informs us, looking like a wise little owl behind his horn-rims.

I squint at him. "What's a flying butthead?"

"Very funny," Charlie says. "It's an architectural term. A buttress shores up an exterior wall and adds stability."

My little brother, the encyclopedia.

So, on a large tray at the dining room table, we build a Gothic gingerbread cathedral with flying buttresses, pointed arches, and a "rose window" made out of a double-layer cookie with raspberry jam in the middle. The top layer has a star shape cut out of it.

When we finish, everyone applauds.

"Well done," says Rebecca, twisting her hair into a knot

on top of her head and securing it with a couple of chop-sticks. She looks stunning, her dark olive skin set off by a deep green cashmere sweater.

Rita takes a picture of our gingerbread masterpiece with her smart phone. "It looks like Notre Dame." As soon as she snaps it, the round cookie falls off the facade and rolls off the tray onto the dining room table.

"It looks like lunch," Evan says, popping the cookie into his mouth.

"Hey!" I frown at him. "You just ate the rose window."

"Sorry," he says, crunching down. "You can bill me for the damages."

Matthis reaches out and snags a gumdrop "bush" from the "snowy" icing walkway. He chows on it.

"Stop! You two are a menace to gingerbread society."

But Kale grabs a gingerbread girl standing on the cathedral steps and bites her head off. "Yum," he says around the mouthful, grinning.

Then it's a free-for-all. Charlie yanks off the licorice trim around the main doors.

Evan breaks off another window, this one Gothic and made out of white chocolate.

Abby and Rita pluck trees from the landscaping.

Before long, our architectural model looks as if it's been hit by a meteor.

"You've all ruined your dinners," Rebecca scolds halfheartedly.

"What, like you were planning to cook?" Abby rolls her eyes.

Rebecca looks a little sheepish. "That's what bistros

are for. Oh, is that the telephone?" She excuses herself, glad to shift the focus away from her lack of domesticity.

Evan gently pulls me on top of him for a kiss, trying not to hurt my ribs. I'm laughing, trying—not too hard— to get away from him, when Rebecca returns looking serious. She turns off the music, and the sudden silence is grating. Just like that, our Christmas is suspended.

"Kari. Charlie."

I slide off Evan and stand up. "Yes?"

"There's a lead on the location of the KGB2 cell."

The gingerbread and candy that I've eaten hardens into an indigestible ball in my stomach. "Oh."

"We're going after them. Do you and Charlie want to be part of the operation?"

Evan inhales audibly and then swears under his breath.

I can't breathe. Do I want to hunt down my parents, confront them, and get a full explanation of what they're up to? Of course.

Do I want them to be caught, imprisoned, and maybe worse? No, I can't say that I do.

My eyes go to Charlie. I think about everything we've just been through. I think about how the Russian "doc" wanted to kill us, even though Charlie is only seven years old. Am I willing to risk his life again? Just for some answers?

My brother turns his gaze on me and sees clearly that I'm waffling. So he takes the decision out of my hands. "I'm in."

"Charlie, it's not up to you," I say, trying to soften the words with a gentle tone.

He raises his chin. "It's fifty percent up to me. They're my parents too. And I'm *in*."

I take a deep breath, shooting an apologetic glance to Evan, who looks pale and tense. He shakes his head and mouths the word "no."

I turn to Rebecca. "When do you need an answer?"

She gives me a level stare. "Soon. Very soon."

I walk to the hall closet to grab my coat and a scarf. "I need to get some air and think about it. I'll let you know when I get back."

She nods.

I go to the door and hesitate before pulling it open. After all, I don't really know what's beyond it.

None of us ever do.